David, viscount Waverly, stirs emotions in Hope that she has never felt.

"Now then," David put his arms about Hope, holding her a trifle more closely than strictly conventional, "I shall dance with the prettiest girl here."

Hope tried to appear merely polite, "I am sure you jest , but thank you anyway."

"But you are, Hope. You are a lovely person inside and out, and I have every intention of getting better acquainted."

"Pretty?" she inquired.

David thought she sought further flowery compliments until he looked down into her pain-filled eyes. Missing a step, he stopped, took her arm, and led her from the floor. "It's a beautiful October evening. Will you walk with me in the garden?"

Hope could only nod and follow David out in the cool night air. A light breeze rippled her golden curls, and she breathed in the fragrance of the late-blooming flowers and pungent herbs. "It is a wonderful night," she sighed, then blushed for it was the young man at her side who made it wonderful.

Silently David turned her to face him. A moment later his lips softly touched hers. Hope thought her heart stopped beating, then it pounded in her chest until she thought she might faint.

"Oh, David," she breathed once he released her. "You mustn't."

A wry smile twisted

and once more capture

CAROLYN R. SCHEIDIES makes her home in Nebraska with her husband Keith and their two children. Carolyn is active in her church's puppet ministry as well as the pro-life movement. She writes inspirational romance because "what better way to help someone know God's love than through the eyes of characters who live it."

Books by Carolyn R. Scheidies

HEARTSONG PRESENTS
HP94—To Be Strong
HP160—To Keep Faith

Where There is Hope

Carolyn R. Scheidies

The Bonds of Love

Heartsong Presents

To my children, Christopher (Chris) and Cassandra (Cassie), with my love. I am both humbled and thankful for their desire to be all that the Lord wants them to be.

HOPE
His love,
Greater than
Betrayal or despair.
His grace,
Sufficient as I
Place my trust in Him.

A note from the Author:
I love to hear from my readers! You may write to me at the following address:
Carolyn R. Scheidies
Author Relations
P.O. Box 719
Uhrichsville, OH 44683

ISBN 1-55748-912-2

WHERE THERE IS HOPE

Cover illustration by Victoria Lisi.

PRINTED IN THE U.S.A.

one

1833

Tucking a stray golden curl under the worn floppy hat, Hope Forrester glanced back at the gothic keep standing dark against the rays of the nearly full moon.

"Farewell," she whispered to the dark structure with its hideous gargoyles grinning down at her plight, making her shudder. Why ever had her father purchased the ancient structure?

For a moment, tears stung her hazel eyes as she thought of her large, good-hearted father. If only he hadn't died so unexpectedly in that accident, she wouldn't now be forced to flee the only home she had ever known.

Tightening her grip on the worn valise in her hand, she turned and resolutely headed away from Forrest Hall, away from Mrs. Forrester, her manipulative, social climbing mother, and, most of all, away from Sir Arland Beaucamp.

Losing herself in the shadow of the tall oak, Hope set off down the darkened roadway secure in the knowledge that at this time of night no one would be up and about. And who would deign to notice a young lad who dressed and smelled of the stable? A faint smile played over Hope's full lips as she sniffed herself. She smelled of horses, a smell she never had minded before. Then again, she had never had such a close acquaintance with their odor.

As the morning sun threw its rays over the countryside, Hope paused, letting the light bathe her clear, soft cheeks in its warmth. Still and all, the late summer air remained chill, and she kept the old cloak pulled tightly about her shoulders as she continued on. An hour later the sound of hoofbeats sent her clattering into the trees where she remained hidden until the sounds faded into the distance.

It would have been easy for her to catch the stage to Leeds and then south at the nearby posting inn, but they knew her there, and her disguise would have done little but get her sent directly home. Now as her stomach growled, she wished she had thought to bring something on which to snack, but it was too late for regrets.

Tired from a night without sleep and several hours of walking, Hope stopped and, keeping carefully out of sight of the road, sat down near a hedge row. Though she had always enjoyed walking over the carefully tended estate her father long ago purchased from a done-up peer, she had never walked so far before, and even in her sturdy walking boots, her feet ached. Talking off her left boot, Hope rubbed her heel, feeling the start of a blister.

For a moment she leaned back and closed her eyes, only to be awakened by a sharp bark and a cold wet nose against her cheek. Grimacing at the slobbery kisses, Hope pushed the black and yellow puppy away from her. "All right." Scratching the ugly mutt between the ears, she scolded him. "Now you get on home. Go."

His hangdog look tugged at her soft heart, but she had no time for the dog now. Both heard the far off call. "Belcher. Here, Belcher."

Pricking up his ears, the dog glanced once more at Hope before bounding away with a joyful cry. Relieved, Hope picked up her valise and, with a sigh, continued on her way, careful to avoid any horses and vehicles which passed.

By mid-morning the sun had grown too warm for her

cloak, and she flung it back over her shoulder. Her valise hung like lead on her sore wrist, and her feet ached. The blister burst into an open sore which rubbed the back of her boots at every step. Her stomach growled in time to the crunch of her stumbling feet, and she heartily wished she had thought to pack something more than a change of clothes and other necessities in her bag.

But she wouldn't go back, not to a home that no longer welcomed her; not that she had ever felt wanted by her mother. Somehow her mother's indifference hadn't mattered when Hope had enjoyed the boisterous affection of her father, a country squire who much to the dismay of his wife seldom left his carefully attended estates. He loved his land, his people, and his youngest daughter who was so much like himself.

There seemed almost as little affection between the squire and Hope's mother as there had been between her mother and herself. As she grew older, Hope sensed that her father was actually relieved when her mother set off to take London by storm with her three beautiful older daughters. Annabel, Elizabeth, and Marian were all like their mother: tall, voluptuous, and pretty, very different from the smaller, rounder youngest daughter—though there was a slight family resemblance.

Living in the shadow of her well-endowed sisters, Hope never recognized her own special beauty which went beyond her golden hair and clear soft skin. Compassion and kindness shown from her sparkling eyes which seldom darkened with self-pity.

Grimacing, Hope recalled coming in on a conversation between her mother and a guest. "Hope takes after the Squire's side of the family. Not much looks there, but," she sighed deeply, "I shall do my best for the girl when the time comes. Of course, my dearest wish is for each of the girls to marry up; a title, you know."

Shuddering, Hope hunched her wide shoulders which gave proportion to her body. Her father would never have countenanced the match her mother had in mind, a match geared to increase their holdings and put another title in the family. The thought of Beaucamp's hand on her arm settled her determination, and Hope purposefully continued plodding down the road.

By noon she reached her first destination, the posting inn from which she planned to catch a stage south. No one knew the country squire's daughter here, and the landlord scarcely took time to answer her questions until she counted out the fare and money enough for her first meal of the day.

She forced herself to eat and drink slowly as she sat alone at a grimy table in the far corner of the all-too-public common room. It was interesting to watch her fellow diners, for though she had traveled little, when she had, there had always been servants to do her father's bidding and a private room put at their disposal. Glancing about, she caught a rotund gentleman staring back at her.

He wore a less than fashionable coat of bottle green with a loud, patterned waistcoat. The combination of orange and green was slightly nauseating, and Hope wondered as much at his taste as at his boisterous laughter.

Uneasily, Hope finished her meal, picked up her valise and cloak, and went to wait for the stage. And wait. And wait. A red-faced farmer strode out to gaze up the road, then swore when he could see no sign of the late stage.

Pulling her cloak more firmly about her shoulders, Hope, too, waited impatiently at the posting inn for the public conveyance which would take her south to London. She bit her lip. By now they knew she was gone, for when she did not make an appearance at luncheon, her mother would send someone up to her room. She only hoped they had not discovered her absence sooner. Still every minute here increased her danger of being found out.

"Aye, lad, move over," commanded the rather stout gentleman she'd seen inside.

"I beg your pardon, sir," Hope started, then straightened. Blushing she lowered her head hoping the pompous man hadn't noticed her all too polite manners. Tired from her long walk, Hope wished for nothing more than a soft bed and Annie to help her into a soft nightgown.

Rubbing the rough material of the shirt and long pants she had rifled from a stable lad, Hope reminded herself she was no longer a pampered miss, daughter of a country squire. Hope swaggered. "As you wish gov'nor."

"Sly boots," laughed the man, cuffing Hope lightly on the shoulder. "Mr. de Court to you, lad. Harry de Court."

Ruefully she moved back, rubbing her shoulder. Still, her efforts seemed to have won her a dubious protector. "I like your style, young wag." He said congenially and proceeded to regale Hope with a string of untenable tales.

Thankfully she needed do little but nod her head. Other travelers listened a moment, then went about their business, assuming the lad and the older man traveled together.

Just as the stage pulled up with a flourish and the echoing sounds from the yard of tin, Hope recognized the huge chestnut stallion racing toward her. However much she had told herself she had little to fear decked out in used servant's clothing, she well knew her face would give her away to the dark-haired, dark-faced, heavy handed Corinthian swinging from the saddle.

The gentleman at her side noted the tightening of her lips, the fear in her eyes. "Runaway are you?" he asked softly.

"Reward out for ya, young scamp?"

"Please, sir," Hope whispered through trembling lips, "don't give me away."

"It is Sir Arland Beaucamp, is it not?"

Hope nodded. With a decided gleam in his slightly protruding eyes, Harry surveyed the nob striding toward the door. "Yes, I know of him," he growled. "He's a cruel master, I own."

With Sir Beaucamp marching toward her and the man at her side suspicious, Hope could only stand in horror, waiting for the elegant Beaucamp to pounce and drag her back home.

Lord, help me, she cried out in her heart. *I can't bear to go back with him. I'd rather die than marry him, whatever Mama says. You know he doesn't really want me.*

She flushed, remembering the glimpse she'd had of him the day after he asked for her hand. She had discovered him in the barn with one of the kitchen maids. Not that his behavior had been unexpected, but hearing about his exploits with women had been far different from witnessing it. She shuddered involuntarily at the memory.

When she'd confronted him, he'd merely laughed off his dalliance, and her mother had scolded her!

Expecting to feel his hateful hand on her shoulder, Hope was surprised to find herself thrust aside by the florid gentleman. "Pardon, M'lord," he crowed, "My lad is a bit of a slow top." Taking Hope by the arm, he hurried her to the stage. "We mustn't be tardy, lad. Long way to go."

From her seat on the coach, Hope heard Beaucamp's bellowing command. "I want information, and I want it now. I am looking for a young lady, seventeen years, average height, average looks, a bit on the plump side, blonde hair, hazel eyes. Come man. She had to go through here. There isn't another stage for miles, and I have tried all the others. I know she is headed to London, and I shall find her if I have to go all the way to London."

Hope flushed under the slow perusal of her rescuer. "Umm," was all he said as he leaned back against the dusty squabs and went to sleep. But burned into Hope's mind was the image of the page of the London *Gazette* in Beaucamp's hand. Was it the very same she ripped out but forgot to bring—the section advertising a domestic bureau?

"Please, Lord, don't let it be that." To quell the panic welling up inside, Hope forced herself to study her fellow passengers.

Beside her a farmer's wife held a basket in one arm and tried to keep a toddler quiet with the other. Heels drummed overhead along with cries from the cup shot bucks on the roof to the coachman. "Get along or let me handle the ribbons."

Hope could only pray he would not agree. She well knew the number of accidents caused by foxed gentleman taking over the driving of a passenger coach. But as the coachman increased his speed, the cries died down to raucous laughter.

Closing her eyes against her fear, Hope silently placed her life in the hands of the only One she had been able to trust since her father's unexpected demise. Her lips tightened and she determined not to think about that, not now.

If only it had happened before her sisters had all married. She well knew Marian, at least, would have gladly welcomed the handsome baron's suit. When Hope commented on her match with the elderly earl, Marian shook her long dark curls. "Dear sister, how naive. Surely you do not believe I am marrying that dottering old man for *love?*"

"How can you say such a thing about the man you are going to marry? He's kind, even if he is rather. . ."

"Ancient," her sister relied repressively. "But who cares.

Once I am married, I shall take my place in society and spend all his lovely money."

"He wants to live on his country estate, like Father."

Marian wrinkled her nose in distaste. "Such a green goose you are. You don't really expect me to bury myself in the country."

"Then how could you accept him, Mary?"

"For his title and deep pockets, of course. Why else?" Patting her latest acquisition, a hand-embroidered gown from Bond Street, Marian sighed. "Tis a shame Arland didn't come up to scratch, but then I hear he's sitting in the pocket of a highly placed lady." She glanced slyly toward her sister. "If you know what I mean."

Hope had no idea, but resisted the temptation to question her sister, knowing it would only bring her sister's ridicule down on her head. Silently giving thanks Arland was not going to become part of the family, she fetched her sister's shawl from the large mahogany armoire.

Well, Arland had come up to scratch, but much too late for Marian. Hope well knew why he lowered himself to ask for her hand when he had little respect for her. With all her sisters married well and with no direct heir, her father had left Hope not only the estate, but also most of his wealth—all of which was under her mother's direction until she was twenty-one or married. As usual, Beaucamp's pockets were to let, and while her mother was doing her best to dissipate the family coffers, Arland would certainly finish off Hope's respectable portion.

When her mother sent her into the parlour all got up in a yellow gown with a neckline which brought embarrassed color to her cheeks, Hope had not missed the grimace on Arland's face as she walked toward him or the disdain in his eyes as he bespoke for her hand in such honeyed, well-practiced flummery, Hope was hard put not to giggle.

Instead she smiled sweetly. “Thank you for your generous offer, Arland, but I fear we will not suit. Though you and my sisters always got along famously, you and I have been on the outs since the day you ran down my puppy.”

“Still recall that, do you? ’Twas but a boyish prank, and you are far too old to hold a grudge.”

“Boyish prank? To deliberately run down a pet? No, I will not forget. Nor will I forget the harsh way you treat your tenants.” She jutted out her chin. “I’m glad the Whigs passed the Reform Bill last year.”

Hope moved away from the touch of his hand. He followed her across the room to the tall window overlooking the gardens. “Your mother has already given her permission, Hope. I don’t need yours.” His hands tightened on her bare arms, and he swung her to face him. The look in his eyes frightened her.

“Arland, you are hurting me.”

His smile chilled her. “We shall deal well together, my dear. If you don’t kick up a fuss over this, that is. It shall go ill with you if you continue to fight me, for I shall delight in taming you.”

“I suppose you’ll beat me like you do your horses.” She spat out, then started at the gleam in his eyes. “I’ll not marry you,Arland, not ever!” Picking up her overlong skirts, she ran from the room, almost tripping in her haste to get away.

Though she pleaded with her mother, Hope found Mrs. Forrester adamant in her stand. “You shall marry him, daughter, whatever you say. You are underage and in my control.”

“I will not marry Arland. I have never liked him. He is rag-mannered,”

“Only toward you, dear.”

“He is cruel and arrogant.”

"He is a lord with open doors to the very best families."

"He is a skirt chaser."

Mrs. Forrester fanned herself rapidly. "That is quite enough, daughter. The man is unmarried, and if he has discreet liaisons—"

"Discreet? The man is overfamiliar with every young woman in the county, whether or not she welcomes his advances. Then there are the married women."

They argued for over a week. Finally, her mother threw a party and, without Hope's prior knowledge, announced the betrothal. Both Beaucamp and Mrs. Forrester had every intention of hurrying the engagement to a quick conclusion.

Hope sucked in a deep breath. She had spiked their guns by running away. She absolutely would not marry a man who both frightened and disgusted her.

Tears stung her closed lids, and Hope raised a trembling hand to wipe them away. Hatred vied with deep sadness. Glancing out the window, she said good-bye to the innocent girl she had left behind. Resolutely she put her memories behind her and faced the bleak future, her future. Once in London she was certain she would be able to find work as a companion or governess. All she need do was sign on with a domestic bureau.

Since she'd been in leading strings, her mother and sisters had drummed into her mind her obvious lack of feminine attributes, her lack of height and gracefulness, her less than slender body. At least she wouldn't be a threat to the peace of the mistress of any house in which she worked. Hopefully she also would not attract the unwanted attentions of any males in the household.

Her rescuer did not awaken until the coachman sounded the yard of tin at the next stop. With a grunt, he opened his eyes. A moment later, Hope found herself propelled by his arm from the coach to the inn. As the hostlers changed the carriage horses, the weary travelers sat down to the refreshments plopped on the table before them by the harried serving girl dressed in a thin, soiled gown.

There was scarcely time for Hope to grab a bite and drink her cider before the summons sounded for the passengers. How different this was from the leisurely well-planned trips as the squire's daughter. With a sigh, Hope allowed Harry to help her back into the coach. His ragged breathing concerned her, and she had no intention of causing him trouble. The seat beside her was now taken by a gaunt cleric in a dark shiny suit which had seen much better days. Still, his tired eyes smiled at her kindly, and Hope felt a certain peace at his presence.

After a comfortable silence, Hope's curiosity forced the question. "Are you from around here, Reverend?"

"Reverend Sanders. No, I had to return to my home." His lips tightened. "My younger brother died."

Flushing, Hope cursed her run-away tongue. "I. . .I'm sorry."

The cleric tried to make her feel more at ease. "It's all right. Richard has always been sickly. Still it is difficult, even when I know he goes to a better place." He smiled sadly.

"And now you are on your way back to your church."

"Yes." Leaning his weary head against the thin cushions, the cleric slept.

When they stopped for the night, Hope tensed. She had paid for a room, but when the landlord assigned her with several other male passengers, fear flared in her eyes. Heaving his considerable bulk forward, Harry claimed a single room. "The lad is with me," he said, grasping her arm in a surprisingly strong grip.

Not knowing what else to do, Hope followed him up the

stairs. Once in the room, a small chamber with an even smaller bed, Hope gasped in dismay. “I can’t stay here. . . with you. I can’t.”

“Because you are of the female persuasion?” de Court asked with a decided smile.

Again fear flared and she backed up. “I. . .how? You heard Arland.”

“Arland is it.” He frowned. Hatred flashed in his eyes, then dulled into pain. “He is an evil man. Child, if you think of me as a man of his stamp, you do me great insult.”

“You. . .you won’t. . .hurt me?” Hope swallowed, trying to read the man’s face. “Then why?”

He shook his head. “I well know you are a gently bred lady.” He ignored Hope’s gasp. “And, no, I would never, ever give over a woman of whatever station into the claws of that lecher.”

“You *do* know him.”

“Indeed I do,” de Court growled.

“But this room. . . .” Hope glanced at the bed and away.

“You’ll have to trust me, child. I am a man who lives by my wits, but I have never forced myself on any woman, not ever. You are safe enough with me. You’ll take the bed.”

“And you?” Hope was overwhelmed by his kindness.

Harry laughed. “I’ll be downstairs trying to do the locals out of their hard-earned money.”

At Hope’s frightened stare, he shook his head. “Cards, lass. I play cards. I make my living, such as it is, with cards. You’ll have the room all to yourself.”

After the substantial dinner he made certain Hope ate, Harry, true to his word, left her the room. Still cautious, Hope climbed into bed without undressing. Exhausted from the hours of walking and even longer hours of being tossed about in the coach, she fell into a deep sleep.

Harry shook her awake the next morning. "Come on. You're late. If you don't hurry, the stage will leave without us." He waddled toward the door. "You have ten minutes, then meet me downstairs."

Hope made it with a minute to spare. She had time to gulp down half a glass of cider and stuff a hard biscuit in her mouth, before Harry propelled her outside. Once the rush was over, Hope leaned back against the squabs. Her heel burned from the open sore and she worried it might get infected, but there was little she could do.

Once more the cleric rode with them along with a wiry little man who squeezed beside Harry's bulk opposite her. From the moment he sat down, the little man never stopped talking. He was a salesman with an exhausting enthusiasm for his product—chocolate. He even passed around samples which helped make him a little less irritating.

The hours dragged by, and the coach made fairly decent time along dusty hard-packed roads—at least so the cleric claimed, and Harry agreed in that choking gasp that so concerned Hope. She said as little as possible and slept.

They passed through Yorkshire, Nottingham, Leicestershire. Each night, Hope thankfully took Harry's bed while he played cards. By the time they stopped in Northampton, Harry seemed tired and out of sorts. If anything, his breathing was more labored than ever. Hope was convinced he meant her no personal harm and begged him to sleep that night in the room.

"There's a couch here," she said, "I'll sleep on that. Please, Harry, you don't look well."

He just shook his head. "No, dear. After all those yokel stops, think you I will pass up a chance to take money off these city folks with much deeper pockets?"

"But Harry. . ." Hope's pleas went unheeded, and he left

her as he had the other nights.

Gingerly taking off her boot, Hope reflected that she did not feel quite the thing either. The sore on her heel had widened and deepened and looked angry and red. Soaking it eased it somewhat, but Hope worried about what would happen if she sickened. She could not depend on Harry forever. Besides, he was not going on to London right now.

Sleep came slowly that night, and Hope was just drifting off when a knock came at the door. "It's me, lad. Open up." coughed Harry.

Swinging out of bed, Hope winced as her heel hit the floor. Hobbling over to the door, she admitted her friend. "Harry, what is it? What's wrong?"

Breathing heavily, Harry waddled into the room, letting Hope shut and lock it after him. Quickly lighting a candle, she glanced at de Court's ashen face. "Harry!" She grabbed his arm and helped him sit down on the couch. "You're ill."

A weak smile stretched his lips. "I fear so, dear." he coughed, sucking up air.

"What's wrong? What can I do to help? I'll have the landlord call the doctor."

He grabbed her arm. "No, miss, ain't nothing you can do. It's my lungs. Heart, too. Doctor warned me often enough to take it easy, settle down."

"Harry," Hope wailed.

"Oh, I'll be all right. Just need to rest." He smiled rathersadly. "Would you talk to me?"

"Of a certain," said Hope as she pulled up a rather decrepit ladderback chair and sat down.

Reaching out, he groped for her hand and held it tightly to his chest. "My dear, I am worried about you." His gurgle of laughter ended in a coughing fit which badly frightened Hope.

"Harry, let me find a doctor. Please."

"No, child. Just listen to me. I'm worried about you. You need someone to take care of you." At her look he hastened to add. "No I won't send you back to *him."*

"Harry, I know he is a horrid man, but why do you hate him so?"

The hand on hers tightened. With a deep rasping cough he began. "Child, that. . .that horrible man ravished my youngest sister, then discarded her as though she were no more than a dog. My sister. . .she was. . .only fifteen."

Hope's face paled. "Oh, Harry, how awful!"

"I'll not send you back to him. But I cannot leave you unprotected, either."

"Don't talk like that. Harry, I'll be fine. I know I'm no beauty, so I doubt I'll have much trouble with, with that kind of gentleman. Arland is different. He has other reasons for offering me his name. In London I'm going to go to a domestic bureau where I am sure to find respectable work."

Slowly, de Court nodded. "You have no idea of your loveliness, my dear. I've been no saint in my life, but I've not preyed on the innocent, either. And I will not let you gallivant off without some protection."

"Please don't worry about me, Harry. God will take care of me. I prayed for protection, and He sent you."

"An unlikely angel, at best." A smile touched his lips. "When you get to London, I want you to promise me something."

"If I can."

"I want you to go to my sister and tell her I said to watch out for you. She's a good woman, a widow. She's often lonely and she'll like your company."

"But I—"

"Promise me this."

"All right, Harry. When I get to London, I shall look up your sister. Where do I find her?"

Harry repeated the name and address until Hope had it firmly committed to memory. "Now, will you bring Reverend Sanders here?"

"Harry, you're not. . ."

"Just fetch him, child. And hurry."

The cleric responded to Hope's frantic summons and was soon by Harry's side. "You need a doctor, de Court."

"No, there's no hope for me now, Reverend. I need you. There are some things I must get straight with Him." A coughing spell overcame Harry, and it was several minutes before he could continue.

Leaving her friend his privacy, Hope walked over to the window and stared out over the stable yard. Shivering in the chill air blowing through the ill-fitting frame, she prayed for God's touch of healing on her friend. In the background she heard the low murmur of voices. Finally, silence.

"Lad," called Sanders. "It's all over. He's gone."

Running to Harry's side, Hope flung herself beside him. "No, no it can't be. I prayed God would heal him."

Sanders put a comforting hand on her shoulder. "Look at his face, lad. God did heal him. He took him home."

Hope could not deny the look of serenity on the face of her new friend. Tears flowed then, not for Harry, but herself. For the first time since leaving Beaucamp behind, Hope was genuinely frightened.

The next couple of days, the minister stayed with Hope, smoothing the way as they buried Harry. With his characteristic kindness, Harry had left his winnings with her so Hope had money for the inn and for a coach to London.

As the time came, the Reverend Sanders left reluctantly. He was not sure why leaving the lad troubled him so. Once again he tried to persuade Harry's companion to travel with him. "Why not come with me to Cambridge? I am sure I can find work for you."

Hope shook her head. She, too, hated to part with the good minister, but wondered just how sympathetic he would be should he discover her ruse. "Thank you, Reverend Sanders, but Harry said I was go to his sister in London."

"All right then, lad. God bless."

It was not easy for Hope to board the coach south alone, but in her guise, no one gave her a second glance—though she was not always given the best accommodations. Part of the day she had to ride on the roof and hold on tightly so as not to be thrown off when a young buck took the reins.

That night she slept in the hay rather than with the other young men taking rooms for the night. The hay was clean and smelled more sweetly than her clothes. A stable cat kept the mice at bay by curling up at her side. Hope awoke groggy and warm, but ready to travel.

Her heel was festered and throbbed constantly, making it difficult for her to sleep on the swaying carriage. Recent rains had turned the roads muddy, and the horses strained to pull the heavy, overloaded coach. Hope hated hearing the coachman shout at the hapless horses and flinched at the frequent sound of the whip.

Wearily she managed to get through her days as the coach wound its way to Bedford and on to Hertford. Each day she felt more exhausted. Each day she grew warmer. She had never realized how much the weather changed from north to south. Doubt nagged her. Was it, in truth the weather? She put a shaking hand to her forehead. It felt hot to the touch. Well, no matter. Before long she would be in London, where hopefully Harry's sister, Mrs. Meintor, would help her.

That night, rain turned the roads into a quagmire, but still the coachman insisted on continuing. Her money running out, Hope was thankful she did not have to stay at an inn for another night. But a few hours from town, the coach crashed onto its side. Screaming passengers climbed from the overturned vehicle into the rain, which descended in torrents.

Blinded by the rain and confused, Hope wandered away from the others. The more she tried to find them, the more confused and wet she became. In her dazed state, she was not certain how far she walked. She began to sneeze. Her body shook. All that night and the next day, it rained. Though she tried to find shelter, Hope found nothing and stumbled on.

That night she found shelter under a large tree. The trunk felt warm against her back as she balled up for warmth. How she wished for even the warmth of hay and a half-wild cat. She had wanted to die rather than marry Beaucamp. Mayhap she would get that wish.

"Lord, help me," were her last coherent words.

❧

Mrs. Haskle, housekeeper for the marquess of Aven, sighed. Once more the cart stuck in the deep mud of the narrow road. Her sister, now recovering from birthing a large healthy son, begged her to stay, but once the rain let up after two solid days, Mrs. Haskle, who not only loved her work, but also took her responsibilities seriously, insisted on starting for Ravenhill.

The boy with her jumped down to free the wheel when a sodden lump of clothes arrested his attention. "Miz Haskle," he cried. "Someone's dead here."

The heavy-set woman sighed and set her feet down, trying to avoid the worst of the muck. Kneeling down, she turned over the lump. The lad burned with fever and seemed oblivious to his surroundings. Mrs. Haskle never could send away a needy soul.

"Come lad, pick up the child. We'll take him to Ravenhill."

two

Faith Glynis, the marchioness of Aven, rode up with her daughters, Celeste and Gwen, as the housekeeper turned in the drive.

"What do you have there, Mrs. Haskle?" asked Gwen curiously.

"'Tis a lad Dan, here, found alongside the road. Burning with fever, he is."

Dan pulled up at the side entrance and stopped. Dubiously Faith eyed the ragtag bundle in the housekeeper's strong arms. Swinging down, she approached Mrs. Haskle. "A contagion, mayhap." She felt the lad's forehead, noting the soft complexion, the fine bone structure. "Girls, don't come any closer, just in case."

"But I want to know—" Gwen protested. Celeste silenced her younger sister with a look.

"Mother, you will satisfy our curiosity later?" asked Celeste from her grownup fifteen years.

Faith spared a smile. "Later," she said, following Mrs. Haskle through the door and into the large open area which opened into the kitchens and to the staircase to the servants' quarters.

"Go about your business," commanded Mrs. Haskle as she passed maids and footmen who turned to stare at them. With a grunt, she led the way up the narrow stairs.

"Isn't he heavy for you?"

"I'll manage," huffed the sturdy housekeeper, entering a

narrow room with a single bed. "Better than risking contagion spread."

After laying the lad down on the bed, Mrs. Haskle pulled off the boy's boots while Faith reached for his jacket.

"Milady, stand back. You must take care not to get too close."

"Fustian! The lad is ill, and I am here."

"His lordship would never forgive me should something happen to you." Pulling off the worn filthy socks, the housekeeper gasped. "Look at this. This heel is like raw meat. . . and infected."

"Then he. . ." Faith echoed the housekeeper's gasp as she pulled off the jacket and shirt. "She! Mrs. Haskle, this is a girl."

"And gently bred from the looks of it. A runaway, I suspect."

"A young lady." Staring at the girl, Faith sensed a certain bond with her.

"Yes, ma'am."

Her lips firm, Faith decided. "Then let's get her downstairs."

"But, milady, we know nothing about her."

"I have a feeling, Mrs. Haskle."

The housekeeper grinned, well knowing the special link which made her mistress and the marquess all but read each other's minds. "I know, milady. Far be it from me to argue with yer feeling."

Together, they moved Hope downstairs, bathed her, and put her into one of Celeste's nightgowns. When Dr. Meyer arrived, the girl lay between clean sheets on a four poster bed in the jonquil room.

Faith had to smile at the spare young man who peered

through his glasses rather like an owl. Though very different from his retired, portly father, he had proved himself most competent.

With a mutter at the angry wound on his patient's heel, Dr. Meyer went to work. Afterward he turned to the marchioness. "The heel is bad, but we've let out the poison. The girl also has pneumonia and will need to be watched closely."

After he left them, with particular instructions for her care, Mrs. Haskle assigned Jenny to care for the girl.

"She knows how to keep a tight lip, and she's had lots of experience with all those children of hers. She brought the littlest one through a worse bout than this three years ago."

Gwen and Celeste, excited at the mystery surrounding the girl, took their turn at her bedside, hoping she would awake while they stood watch.

"I'll bet she's a runaway princess," said nine-year-old Gwen, whose mind was filled with fairy tales.

"Oh, phooey. She is a silly goose to run off. Think of all the dreadful things which might have happened to her."

"She's running from an evil prince who wants to marry her and lock her away forever in his dungeon."

"Really," said Celeste archly, "what an imagination."

"Ouch. You sound just like Miss Browne." Gwen let out a long sigh. "I would never have believed she could be so romantic as to go off and marry that vicar after corresponding all those years."

"It was about time we graduated from a nanny," commented her older sister dryly.

"Ah, come on, Celeste. Miss Browne was more a governess than a nanny to you anyway."

Still Celeste was almost as excited as Gwen when a couple

days later their mother informed them the fever had broken and the girl was awake. "Wonderful!" cried Gwen, clapping her hands. "Let's go up. I must find out who she is."

"Hold it young lady," cautioned Faith. "You'll have to wait until the doctor gives his approval. Until then, neither of you is to go into her room. Is that clear?" Though she spoke to both girls, her eyes were on Gwen.

The younger girl pouted. "Botheration!"

Hope awoke in a large bed hung with forest green velvet curtains edged with bright yellow tassels. Blinking, Hope put a hand to her throbbing head trying to recall how she came to be in this lavish setting. Ruffles circled her thin wrists.

Her eyes widened in consternation at the decidedly feminine nightgown. What had happened? Where was she? How had they discovered her gender?

Her cheeks flushed. Of course, someone must have undressed her. But who? And when?

With difficulty she recalled the overturned stage, the rain, and her raging fever. She must have passed out. Well, she was awake now, and it was high time she was on her way. Still not thinking clearly, Hope tried to get out of bed only to find that her rubbery legs would not hold her.

Strong arms supported her and helped her settle back down. "There Miss. Must take it easy."

Hope stared up into Jenny's plain, but pleasant face. "Where am I?"

"Ravenhill, miss."

"Ravenhill. Where is that?"

Jenny's eyebrows lifted slightly. "Why in Surrey, miss."

"How long have I been here?"

"Almost on a week now. Mrs. Haskle, the housekeeper,

found you near the road burning with fever from that infected heel and pneumonia. Dr. Meyer be right glad to see you awake."

"Oh," was all Hope could think to say. She dared not ask too many questions of the maid. "Is. . .is there someone with whom I may speak?"

"Yes, miss. The marchioness asked me to let her know the moment you came to. Have to let the doctor know, too."

Fifteen minutes later, the marchioness, gowned in a practical but well-cut gown with a cashmere shawl draped about her shoulders, entered the room. Though of about the same height as Hope, the lady carried herself with a distinctive air that set her apart from the average woman.

This must be the marchioness, Hope decided, liking the softly curved lips, the concerned eyes.

"Miss. . ."

Hope tried to think, but nothing came. "Hope, ah, Forrest." It was almost the truth. "I don't understand how I got here. Your maid said a Mrs. Haskle found me?"

"Yes. Be thankful she did." Faith eyed the young woman. "You want to tell me about it?"

Hope bit her lip. Something about the woman invited confidences, but Hope was too unsure of herself or her present circumstances to fully trust anyone at the moment. If they knew the truth, would they not send her back to her mother . . .and Sir Beaucamp?

Not given to prevarication, Hope stuttered the first thing which came to mind. "I'm dreadfully tired." It was true enough.

For a long moment, Faith studied the young woman. "I am sure you are. I should not have taxed you. Dr. Meyer. . ."

A knock sounded and Faith admitted the doctor.

"How is my patient?"

He squinted through his glasses at the young lady. Hope tried not to smile at the ludicrous sight of the slender doctor peering at her through glasses which persisted on slipping down his thin nose.

The twinkle in his eyes told her he well knew the reason for her amusement. "I can see you are well on the mend young lady. Good." He turned to Faith. "Lady Aven, I doubt you have any more need of my services right now. The young lady is doing fine. I recommend she stays in bed for several more days, then engages in limited activity for a while after that."

With a bow, the doctor picked up his bag and headed out the door. A moment later he popped his head back into the door. "Young lady, I expect you to rest."

Hope could not have agreed with him more. Her eyelids felt decidedly heavy.

"We'll talk again," promised Faith. Something about the girlrang false, and yet, as from the first, she sensed the girl was important to her family.

As the door closed, Hope snuggled back into the covers. Mayhap she could stay a day or two longer. After all, Mrs. Meintor wasn't expecting her. A moment later, Hope slept.

She awoke to a soft giggle. Opening her eyes, she found a young girl peering down at her, while an older girl, about her own age, stood at Hope's shoulder.

"Why hello," Hope said. "Who are you?"

Gwen clapped her hands. "I am Gwendolyn Constance Grace Glynis."

Hope's eyes widened at this recital. The older girl sniffed. "She's in love with her name. . .her whole name, which she recites at every opportunity." The girl smiled, her face open and trusting. "I am Celeste, by-the-by."

"I do not say it all the time!" claimed Gwen. "I just like the way it rolls off my tongue. Rather tickles you know," she said with all the seriousness of a nine-year old. "Do you have brothers or sisters?"

Without thinking, Hope responded to the girl's friendliness. "Three sisters. All older."

"I have two older brothers. They're twins and think they know everything. Jonathan can be quite nice, but Nathaniel—Nate is my favorite. David is nice, too. He brings Dee over to see me lots."

Confused, Hope said, "You said two brothers."

"David is my cousin. His dad is my mother's brother. He married dad's fiancée, you know. She's from Spain, and Celeste is named after her. She is mother's best friend."

This was growing more confused by the second, and Hope applied to the older girl for an explanation.

Celeste giggled. "Gwen, what a muddle. It's like this—Hope, isn't it? Mother said that was your name."

"Yes, please."

"Father brought Aunt Celeste home from the war with Napoleon, but he was really in love with mother. I guess it was a regular mess until Uncle Edmund fell in love with Aunt Celeste and father could marry mother."

Gwen sighed. "It was all sooo romantic."

Celeste rolled her eyes. "That's all she thinks about. I fear her nanny reads her too many fairy tales."

"They're better than those novels you read," spouted Gwen. "If Dad knew you read those. . ."

"You better not tell." Celeste turned to Hope. "What do you think?"

Hope smiled at the exchange. For all the wrangling, the

two girls obviously cared about each other. "I like both fairy tales and some of those novels you're referring too. . .Mrs. Radcliff. But," she added with a sigh, "life is seldom like the stories." Suddenly she felt years older than Celeste and ancient beside the younger Gwen.

"Are you a runaway princess?"

"Gwen, really," admonished her sister.

Hope laughed. "No, I am no princess. Sorry."

"Oh, well," Gwen pulled up a chair and sat down. "I like you anyway."

"It is all right if we stay?" At Hope's nod, Celeste also sat down.

"Who is this Dee?"

"David's youngest sister, Delores. She and Gwen are the best of friends, besides being cousins."

"Oh," said Hope, jealousy bubbled up inside. How she envied this close-knit family. "Do they live close by?"

Celeste nodded. "At Thorn Hall. Their land matches our own. Always going back and forth."

The talk turned more general then. Tiring easily, Hope lay back and listened to the girl's talk. Sometime later, Celeste shushed her sister. "She's asleep again," she whispered. "We'd better leave."

If Hope thought her time in bed would be boring, she reckoned wrong, for the two girls spent much time with her. They talked and laughed and played games until Hope hated the thought of being released from the bedchambers, for then she would have to make plans to continue on to London. The thought was not nearly so exciting anymore.

After spending time with the Glynis sisters and talking further with the marchioness, the desire grew in Hope for a home like this, a home of love and acceptance. A home filled with laughter. But this was not her home, and she could no longer pretend to belong. It was time for her to move on.

Besides, the marchioness continued to ask questions which Hope did not wish to answer. Though she knew her benefactor had every right to know whom she harbored, Hope could not trust anyone that far. Her secret weighed more heavily upon her each day until she felt she could stay no longer without unburdening herself.

Ascertaining from Jenny the location of the nearest stage line, Hope bundled up the clothes Jenny had made over for her from some of Celeste's hand downs. For though Celeste was a couple of years younger, she was taller and more developed than Hope. The clothes also were made to accentuate Celeste's darker coloring, but Hope was grateful for them at any rate.

She touched the pouch around her throat, thankful she had kept Harry's money pouch safely hidden around her neck under her clothes. The marchioness had returned the pouch hoping for an explanation, but when none was forthcoming, she did not insist.

Hope bit her lip, hating to leave. She had not met the marquess, but from all the girls said, he reminded her deeply of her father, a wonderfully caring man. Tears stung her eyes as she lifted the worn travel valise Jenny had dug out for her.

Hope managed to find her way down the stairs and out of the manor without being seen. Furtively, she glanced behind her as she hurried down the drive to the road. She was so worried about being seen, Hope forgot either to watch where she was going or to listen.

Unexpectedly she turned to find herself staring into the faces of chestnuts pulling a carriage at a fast clip. "No!"

she screamed, instinctively raising her hands to protect her face.Why hadn't she heard the carriage coming?

"Move," shouted the coachman, hauling back on the reins with such strength it brought him to his feet, but Hope remained frozen.

Then silence. Had she died? No, she heard the heaving of the horses, the jingle of harness.

"Miss, miss. Are you all right?"

Slowly Hope opened her eyes. "I. . .I think so. I wasn't hit?"

"No thanks to you, miss," growled the anxious coachman. "Why didn't you see us? Or hear us coming?"

Tears started in her eyes and the coachman softened. "'Tis a nasty fright you had miss. Were you on your way to Ravenhill?"

Out of the carriage leaned a slender woman with silver sprinkles in her hair who, though not beautiful in the strict sense of the word, was handsome in her own way.

"Come here, child," the woman commanded. "On the way to Ravenhill. Why I'm headed there myself." Waving a graceful hand, she ordered, "Assist her into the carriage."

Not knowing what else to do, Hope complied as the groom let down the steps and offered her assistance. Her stomach knotted at the thought of returning. What would they think of her, running off after their kindness?

"I am Emily Barrington, from Boston. And you?"

"Hope, ah, Hope Forrest, Ma'am."

The older woman surveyed the girl. "You remind me of my sister-in-law Ada when she was just sixteen." she smiled, but her smile, Hope noted, was sad.

"I am seventeen," she ventured shyly.

"Out gallivanting, just like Ada, I venture."

For some reason, perhaps due to her recent shock, Hope opened up to the woman. "I was on my way to London to get a job."

At the question in the woman's eyes, Hope found herself pouring out her story, concluding, "I don't belong and thought it was time I make it on my own."

As she finished, her eyes widened and she clapped a hand over her mouth. "Oh no. Please, you mustn't tell anyone. If they knew, they must needs return me to my mother."

"Do they know nothing of who you are?"

Hope shook her head. "I. . .I couldn't tell them the whole truth."

"So you left." Emily sat back thoughtfully. "You can't go on with this plan of yours. Not safe, not for a lovely young thing like yourself."

Hope giggled. "Me, lovely? All my life I've been told, except by father, of course, that I have little in the way of looks or other feminine attributes."

"Nonsense," said Emily firmly. "What a hen-witted, and quite untrue, thing to say."

Hope blushed, embarrassed for her mother and sisters. Emily was, of course, simply being kind, yet her matter-of-factness gave Hope pause. Maybe she wasn't as plain as she believed. A spark of hope flared within her breast.

"Now," Emily continued, "we have to decide what tact to take with you. 'Twould be easier if I knew my English relatives."

"Don't you know them?"

"Only through letters, dear. I've never met the marchioness, though I was well acquainted with her father."

"She is a kind person. You will like her, Mrs. Barrington."

"In that case, you follow my lead," Emily said in her take-charge tone which brooked no argument.

As the team pulled up in front of the manor, Emily closed her eyes momentarily, and Hope had the distinct impression she offered up a prayer.

Reluctantly, Hope entered Ravenhill on the heels of the American relative. Taking Hope's bag, Emily ordered a servant to take it up to Hope's room. Then, taking Hope's arm, Emily followed Miter to the elegantly appointed drawing room where the marchioness awaited her in a dusty rose, wingbacked chair. A warm breeze wafted in through the tall windows bordered by lightweight rose curtains, sending the fragrance of late summer flowers through the room.

Gracefully, Faith got to her feet and moved forward to welcome her American cousin. "Mrs. Barrington, Emily Barrington." With surprise she noted Hope at Emily's side.

"I found the child leaving," Emily told the marchioness firmly. "She has some noddy-cocked notion she has worn out her welcome and must find a position."

Hope's cheeks reddened at Emily's betrayal.

The marchioness started. "I had no idea you felt like that, my dear. Of course we don't want you to leave. And going off on your own—it's just not done." Remembering how they found her, she added, "Unless there is something you're running from."

Hope glanced at Emily and was gratified as the older woman shook her head in assurance. Her secret was safe. "Take my word for it, my lady, the child is frightened. It is not easy being young and forced to be on your own. There are wicked people out there ready to take advantage of the young."

The edges of Faith's lips twitched. "Of a certain. Well, there is little need to go into that now. Hope, I am hurt you did not trust me, but I think I understand. Still, I would like your promise you will not go off again without telling us."

Staring down at the toes of shoes passed on from Gwen, Hope nodded slowly. "I. . .I didn't mean to worry anyone. I thought you'd be happy to see me gone. And I wanted to earn my own way."

"Hope Forrest. Celeste is thrilled to have a friend, and Gwen adores you. They would be crushed to think you ran away without even saying good-bye."

Hope gulped. "I never thought of that. Truly, I am sorry, but I do not feel right about doing nothing to earn my keep."

"For now we shall say no more of this. I would rather the girls not know the truth of the matter. Celeste is so trusting, and Gwen, well, Gwen has you cast in a most romantic light."

"Thank you, milady." Hope was relieved when Faith turned her attention to her visitor.

Taking Emily's hand, Faith led her to the divan. "Hope, please pull the bell cord to summon Miter."

Hope did as she was told, then hesitated. "Milady, do you want me to go on to my room?"

"Of course not, Hope. Please stay."

Before she could take a seat, dark-haired Jonathan rushed into the room. "I heard our American cousin was here."

His mother motioned him over. "Jonathan, may I make you acquainted with Mrs. Barrington."

Taking her manicured hand, he bowed. "At your service, Ma'am. Your letters almost prompt me to visit your fair land." Releasing her hand he turned. His smile broadened at the sight of Hope, whom he had not met. "And who do we have here? Not another cousin?"

Hope blushed when he took her hand. "Hope," introduced the marchioness, "may I make you acquainted with my son,

Jonathan. Jonathan, Hope Forrest."

He grinned. "Ah, our mystery guest. Gwen has spoken volumes about you, not to mention Celeste."

Hope blushed even harder. "Nice to make your acquaintance, my lord."

"Jonathan, please." He sat down in a high back chair next to her.

"Son, I can see you are quite taken with our younger guest, but would you please go tell your father our American guest has arrived?" Faith grinned mischievously, "Why not make our other guest a surprise?"

Leaping to his feet, Jonathan grinned back. With a bow to the ladies, he excused himself.

The marquess was all that was gracious as the marchioness introduced him to both Hope and Emily. Once again, every one sat down. Behind her hand, Hope stifled a yawn which went unnoticed until it was echoed by Emily, who apologized profusely. "I fear I have got very little sleep recently. Accommodations were not the best last night."

Getting to her feet, the marchioness eased the way not only for Emily to go up to her room, but also for Hope who slipped up to her room with a sense of relief. The look in Jonathan's eyes discomfited her even as his admiration stirred a longing within her, a longing to be loved for herself, a longing to belong.

Tired, she flung herself across the bed and was soon fast asleep. Jenny woke her much later. "Her ladyship wishes you to come down for luncheon."

Groggily, Hope allowed the maid to dress her in a deceptively simple gown of amaranthus with a white sash and matching pinkish purple ribbons to hold up her cap of natural golden curls. When Jenny turned her to face the mirror, her eyes widened. "You look right nice, if I do say so myself."

Hope could but agree, but when her entrance downstairs prompted Jonathan to hasten to her side with a sincere, "Hope, you look splendid," her heart warmed and she blushed deeply.

Gwen clapped her hands, "You do look better than Celeste did in that gown."

Frowning, Celeste shushed her. "Gwen, what a rag-mannered thing to say."

"I agree," said the marchioness who stood beside Mrs. Barrington.

Large tears welled up in Gwen's eyes. "I didn't mean. . . She *does* look nice."

Emily took charge, "Of course she does, child. No need to cry."

The marchioness froze and the marquess frowned at Emily's forwardness. Hope left Jonathan's side for Gwen. "You are right, Gwen. The dress does become me, and I thank you for your compliment."

"Truly?"

"Truly. It is no secret my things were all lost in the rain."

With a grateful cry, Gwen hugged Hope. "I hope you never go away. Not ever."

A lump in her throat, Hope hugged her back, wishing she could promise Gwen that very thing. At the look in Jonathan's eyes, the thought came unbidden, *You could if you play it right.*

Hiding the dismay on her face against the younger girl's shoulder, Hope rebuked the unworthy thought. She could never use or deceive these people anymore than she already had.

If she had learned one thing from her own family and the relationship between her father and mother, it was the importance of marrying for love, deep abiding mutual love.

As nice as Jonathan was, her heart did not regard him as anything more than a friend.

How badly she wanted to belong. "Help me stay strong, Lord," she whispered.

Dinner was pleasant enough as the family asked questions and Emily told them about their American relatives. Not part of the family, Hope felt she had no right to demand explanations for things she did not fully comprehend. So she listened, storing away her questions.

"My daughter Janice. . . ," Emily said, waving at the footman in a way which brought a frown to the lips of the marquess. Hope doubted Emily realized how she usurped the marchioness's place with her actions. Yet the family was too polite to comment on the situation.

"Janice," prompted Celeste politely, trying, Hope saw, to smooth things over.

"Janice is married, lives in Virginia, and has four children. Course she always did like to mother the other children." She smiled the same sad smile Hope had noticed earlier, and Hope wondered at its cause. "Dane, my son, never did take her bossing him about."

"And is he married?" asked Faith.

Emily hesitated. "Yes. He, too, is married. He took over the family plantation, Hundred Elm. He always preferred working the soil and being with the animals to being with people."

"What about your brother William?" asked Faith. "Was he not also injured in the war?"

"Yes, but he recovered quickly. Will and Ada have three children: Julia, Charity, and little Timothy."

"Did he get his big church?" asked Faith, remembering with some pain even yet her father's letters about the family.

"He did that." Emily frowned. "Now he is talking about

pulling up stakes and taking his family west. He hopes to convertthe heathen Indians. Can you imagine? I can only hope this interest of his will pass with time."

Somehow then the talk turned more general. It was not until they all settled into the parlour that the conversation returned to America. Listening with half an ear, Hope surveyed the large room, from the Adam style ceiling with its delicate carved forms, to the elegant, dusky rose, brocade-covered couch, to the velvet curtains at the large french windows which opened onto a patio.

Gwen's question to the American guest pulled Hope back. "Don't you have another son?"

A faint smile curled Mrs. Barrington's lips, "Ah. Robin, the youngest. Jeremiah," she choked on the name and pain filled her eyes. "Jeremiah left him Boswick Hall, the family home in Boston." Emily stopped then and Hope, sitting next to her, sensed her struggle to continue.

The marquess at her left must have also noticed her struggle. "We were sorry to hear about Jeremiah."

Emily fought for composure. "He struggled for so long. He was a good man, but the pain never left. The injuries he sustained in the war finally overcame him. Robin was devastated that he was not far along in his medical studies to do much good." She smiled weakly. "But Robin is becoming an excellent doctor, and his father was so proud of him. There was really nothing anyone could have done short of a miracle."

Pulling out a handkerchief, Emily wiped tears. "Please," she said getting to her feet, "if you will excuse me."

Faith put an arm about her shoulders. "I understand, Emily. Let me take you to your room." With a start, Faith replayed the time the duchess had done the same for her when news arrived of the death of her father and his new wife, Emily's mother-in-law, Catherine.

The marquess's jaw stiffened as he, too, recalled that agonizing time when he finally admitted his love for Faith had not changed. Hope witnessed a depth of understanding in the man's eyes which surprised her. How she longed for a man with such sensitivity.

Later she scolded herself. Living here was dangerous. Falling on her knees beside her bed, Hope cried, "Lord Jesus. You know how much I want someone to love me like his lordship loves his wife. How I long to be a part of a loving family. But this is not my family, and I feel I must go away. Lord, if You want me to stay, please make it very clear to me."

A verse came to mind: *Trust in the Lord with all thine heart; and lean not unto thine own understanding. In all thy ways acknowledge him, and he shall direct thy path.*

"Show me, Lord, show me."

❧

Several days later, the marchioness had Hope summoned to her sitting room. With trepidation, Hope entered Faith's private domain. "Milady," she curtsied.

"Sit down, Hope," invited Faith from the chair beside the hearth.

Tense, Hope sat stiffly on the edge of the facing deep-cushioned chair. "You wanted to see me?"

"I did indeed. You have been with us now, what is it, three weeks?"

"Yes, milady."

Hope clenched her fists. This was it. The marchioness was giving her marching orders. "I will leave at first light, milady."

"What! Leave. Why ever for? Are you not happy here?"

Hope blinked back tears. "How can you ask such a question?" she burst out. "Of course I love staying here where everyone is so kind. Your. . .your," now she was blubbering and could not stop, "family is so loving to each other. You have a wonderful family."

Faith thought of Nathaniel, but pushed that problem aside momentarily. "If you feel that way, why are you leaving?"

"Because, because. . ." Looking up Hope saw puzzlement and disappointment on the face of the marchioness. "Isn't that why you asked for me? To ask me to leave?"

"Oh, no, dear. The girls would never forgive me." She chuckled kindly. "Quite the opposite. If you are determined to earn you own way," she waited for Hope's determined nod, "then I have the perfect situation in mind."

Hope leaned forward, biting her lip. "Yes?"

"I would you like to be Celeste's companion and Gwen's governess, for now at least, until we can find another. Then you would stay on strictly as Celeste's companion."

"That would be wonderful, but milady, I am scarcely older than Celeste."

"But years older in many ways."

Hope had to agree. Celeste had a trusting openness that Hope had left behind when she ran away from home.

"There is only one thing, Hope. I want you to trust me with the truth."

Hope's shoulder's slumped. It was all over. When the marchioness learned the truth, she would be sent home straightway. Then again, if God wanted her to stay. . .

Taking in a deep breath, Hope began, "For a long time you have suspected I am a runaway, and I am. The reason I ran away is this."

Long after she finished an amended nameless version of her story, the marchioness remained silent, staring into the hearth filled with late blooming flowers.

After an eternity, she met Hope's anxious eyes. "Do you still want the job?"

"More than anything," breathed Hope.

"Then it is yours." Faith paused. "As for the rest, let's wait and see. Mayhap with time you will tell me the whole."

Hope flushed. "Milady."

"Mayhap you will trust me enough to tell me your real name." Faith waited, but Hope remained silent.

With a sigh, Faith said, "All right then, Hope, you may go."

"A. . .and the job?"

A slight smile touched Faith's lips. "I am not in the habit of taking back my promises, Hope."

three

Hope exchanged an amused grin with the duke of Glynmouth, the marquess's father, as Gwen rubbed her brow with hands dirty from helping tend the roses.

From the first, Hope had felt a bond to the old man, strengthened by their special feelings for the energetic Gwen. Hope and Gwen often visited Gwen's grandfather, who had lived in the Dower House since the death of his beloved wife several years earlier.

Hope could scarcely credit that five weeks had passed since the housekeeper hauled her soaked, fever-ridden body to Ravenhill. The days had flown by with lessons, which Hope conscientiously taught, to riding with Gwen and Celeste, to spending time with the family. There were long girl chats with Celeste, and yet always there was a barrier between them. . .a barrier of secrets. It was then she found relief in talking to Emily and grew to care deeply about the older woman who bore so much pain.

Sometimes, of late, Jonathan joined the girls as they rode out for their morning ride. Jonathan, his eyes alight with mischief, teased Hope almost as unmercifully as he did his sisters.

For the first time in her life, Hope felt part of a family—a real family—and she thrust her past to the back of her mind. One day she would have to deal with it, but not now. Every time she opened the Bible, she seemed to read verses about trust and honesty.

Just that morning, she opened it to Leviticus 19 and found, "Ye shall not steal, nor deal falsely, neither lie to one another."

Lord, she cried, *I can't tell them. They'd have to send me home.* With that, she put aside the issue one more time.

Hope had yet to meet the residents of Thorn Hall, of whom she'd heard so much. David had gone to London with his father, the earl of Thorwall, while the rest of the family had gone to Bath hoping the waters would help their ailing daughter, Darla. From the letters sent, Darla appeared to be so much improved that the countess was planning to return to Thorn Hall in a fortnight. Lord Thorwall and David were also expected.

Faith smiled happily at the news, suggesting, "Girls, how would you like to have a party welcoming them back and celebrating Darla's return to health?"

Celeste whirled about, her pale gold gown eddying around her trim ankles. "How about a ball?"

Faith witnessed the hope flash in Hope's eyes and nodded. "If you girls will agree to make out the invitations and oversee the decorations."

"La, Mother, we'll do that—won't we, Hope?"

The next afternoon, the girls commandeered Jonathan to take them into the village for supplies.

Jonathan handled the reins of the open curricle in which the girls rode. The crisp fall air caused Hope to pull her pelisse more closely about her shoulders. Overhead, dark clouds obscured the sun that had been shining so brightly when they left. A moment later, rain drops spattered the shining coats of the bays. Thunder cracked. Restlessly, the bays shied, and Jonathan grimly held onto the reins.

"We have to find shelter," he ground out. "Looks like

we're in for quite the shower."

"Can we make it home?" This from Gwen, huddling under Hope's protective arm.

"Don't think so." Turning the horses, Jonathan let them spring forward on the road. "We're going to Thorn Hall, girls. It's closest."

Despite the thunder, lightning, and pounding rain, Jonathan managed to find his way, pulling up in front of the impressive hall not fifteen minutes later.

The well-trained staff welcomed them. The housekeeper led Celeste and Hope up to the rooms of Celeste's cousin Darla while Delores's nanny took charge of Gwen.

Before long, Celeste and Hope, arrayed in fresh gowns from Darla's closet, surveyed each other and giggled. While Celeste's gown showed a daring amount of ankle, Hope's kept getting under foot. Still giggling, they met Jonathan in the sitting room across the hall where they found tea set out.

Hungry, the trio quickly demolished the sumptuous repast.

Taking a final sip, Hope had the courage to ask, "Do you think your uncle will mind us being here?"

"Not a bit," said Jonathan cheerily, "This is just like home for us. Hey, how about a tour? What say, sis? Shall we show her about?"

Celeste gracefully got to her feet. "I think I will look in on Gwen."

Flushing, Hope hurried to her own feet. "Really. I should do that."

"No need, Hope," Celeste assured her. "You go on. My dear brother is dying to show you about."

With the familiarity and pride of family, Jonathan escorted Hope about. She viewed the green morning room with its classical furnishings. In the library she heard how Jonathan's uncle broke into the Adam designed bookcase with its locked glass doors. But in the family parlor done in warm browns brightened with splashes of colorful tapestries and family portraits, she caught her breath at the portrait over the mantel.

"That's Uncle Edmund and Aunt Celeste and my cousins." He pointed them out one by one. "Delores, the youngest and Gwen's bosom bow. Darla, who is often sick. Daniel, Denby." Admiration shown in his eyes. "And this is David."

As he talked about the cousin he so admired, Hope stared at the picture. She could not keep her eyes from the handsome young man with unruly blond hair and kind laughing eyes, eyes which looked into her heart.

"Handsome, isn't he? What you can't see is the nasty scar on the back of his neck."

"Scar?" Hope asked, licking her dry lips and wondering why her knees felt wobbly.

"Oh, yes. Three years ago, Darla's little mutt tried to run under the wheels of a gig. David threw himself after the silly pup and managed to get himself kicked by the horse for his efforts."

"Did he save the puppy?"

"Of course," said Jonathan, taking her arm. "But it did leave him with that scar." Hope couldn't help but contrast David with Arland Beaucamp.

An hour later as they were able to head home under a cloudless sky, Hope treasured the image of David, who had taken the status of knight in shining armor in her heart.

More than ever, she looked forward to meeting the Fairens on their return and to attending her first grownup ball other than her betrothal ball. The thought of that particular disaster brought a grimace to her face.

Both Hope and Celeste were helping the marchioness plan the welcoming ball for the Fairen's return. But whatever they planned—whether it had to do with decorating, or the menu, or housekeeping—Emily seemed always underfoot, always countermanding orders given by the marchioness until the staff had become sullen and confused. And it didn't stop there.

Mrs. Haskle was in the sitting room with the marchioness, once more complaining about Mrs. Barrington when the marquess stomped into the room, fury darkening his eyes.

"That woman," he said slapping his whip against his dusty riding boots.

Mrs. Haskle hurriedly exited while the Faith went to soothe her husband. "Carter, what is it? What's happened?"

Not seeing the girls working at the desk, he burst out, "You have to do something about Emily. Bother! The woman is determined to undermine my authority."

Faith sighed, "Surely you refine too much on the situation, my dear. I know she is irritating, but—"

"Faith, my darling." The marquess clenched his teeth. "Your Mrs. Barrington just countermanded my direct order to my estate manager. The woman is a meddling menace."

"I had no idea, Carter." Faith grimaced wryly. "I thought she kept busy countermanding *my* orders."

Carter stiffened. "She is causing *you* trouble?"

Celeste stepped forward, "She most certainly is. Cook has threatened to quit, and Mrs. Haskle is barking at everyone."

Taking a seat beside his wife, Carter took her hand. "I think we better have a serious chat with your cousin, my dear. I'll not have your authority questioned."

Biting her lip, Hope hesitantly stood beside Celeste. "Milord, milady. I. . .I think I know what the problem is.

May I speak?"

"Of a certain, child," said the marquess. Though he was kind enough, Hope found him rather distant toward her. How she wished she could tell them the whole truth, but if she did, would they not be honor bound to send her back to her mother? Inside, she ignored the gentle tug at her spirit, *Trust Me.*

"Hope?" This from the marchioness.

"Yes, milady. Mrs. Barrington has been most kind to me. From the first day she came—"

At the marchioness's warning glance, Hope did not go into detail before Celeste. "She and I have talked quite a bit. I think she does not know what to do with herself since the death of her husband. You see, ever since the war, Emily had run the family business affairs and overseen the plantation. True, Dane took on more and more responsibility as he got older, but it wasn't until her husband died that he took over completely. She misses Jeremiah dreadfully, but she also feels lost and unwanted."

Hope bit her lip to keep from adding, "Like I do often enough."

"The poor dear," said Faith. "If I had only known."

The marquess nodded toward Hope. "We have you to thank for pointing this out to us."

"That's because she and Mrs. Barrington spend time together," piped up Celeste. "Mrs. Barrington told me that Hope reminds her of her sister-in-law Ada."

"So, how can we keep the woman busy?" asked the marquess. "However sorry I may be for her plight, I will not brook her interference in my affairs, nor will I allow her to contradict your orders, my dear."

Hope spoke up once again. "Could she not help by taking

food to the poor or helping out at the orphanage, which I understand needs some reorganization?"

Faith smiled. "Why, Hope, those are wonderful ideas. Don't you think so, Carter?"

"It would save having to look into things myself." At the plea in Faith's eyes, he capitulated entirely. Kissing his wife on the nose, the marquess agreed. "I'll take her out this afternoon, but if she can't handle the job. . ."

Faith kissed his cheek. "I know. We'll have to find her something else to do."

Though Celeste seemed to take the open affection between her parents as a matter of course, Hope blushed furiously even while her heart longed for a similar love.

Getting up, the marquess headed for the door. "When I drive Emily over to the orphanage, I'll have a little talk with her."

With Emily happily busy reorganizing the orphanage, the household let out a collective sigh of relief and cheerfully went about readying Ravenhill for the welcoming ball.

"Miss Hope, you're as squiggly as Miss Gwen," Jenny muttered good naturally as she buttoned Hope up in a creation of willow-green silk. The delicate edging of antique lace on the square neckline which dipped modestly in front and banded the lower skirt took attention away from Hope's large shoulders and less than trim waist.

Hope eyed herself in the mirror. "It was nice of Celeste to let us make this over."

Jenny harrumphed. "Generous Lady Celeste is, but she has more gowns than ever she knows what to do with. And this is much more to your coloring than hers."

Hope's attention fell to her waistline. "Well, I am glad there was extra material and that she is taller or there wouldn't have been enough material to let it out."

"Now, Miss Hope. You refine too much on the willowy fashionable ladies." Her hands akimbo on her rather wide hips, Jenny commented wryly, "I rather like your figure."

As the maid intended, Hope giggled. "I guess I shouldn't complain." She inspected herself critically. "Do you really think I look. . .pretty?"

"Quite smashing, if I do say so myself."

Squealing, Hope swung about to find Jonathan languidly leaning against the door frame. "How dare you come in here?"

Straightening, Jonathan grinned. "Ah, fair lady. I found the door all ready ajar."

Bowing, he extended an arm. "Ready, my fair one." He looked every inch the gentleman in his jacket of deep blue superfine, his black breeches, and slippers.

Hope solemnly took his arm. "As you wish my knight in shining armor."

"I'd like to be," Jonathan murmured softly.

Flushing, Hope begged, "Please, Jon, not tonight. Can't we just be friends?"

With an exaggerated sigh, Jonathan sniffed. "As the lady wishes. Tonight we are friends, but tomorrow. . .I pursue in earnest."

Though his tone remained light, Hope discerned a determination behind the words. While she did not believe he was truly serious in his pursuit, he offered a powerful temptation.

Steadying herself, Hope entered the anteroom to the dining hall on Jonathan's strong arm. Her gaze caught the Gainsborough portrait of the marquess's grandfather that hung over the mantel and then fell to the gathered guests.

The crowded room made her want to run back to her room. How could she compete with the elegantly gowned and jeweled ladies laughing together? What right did she, a lowly squire's daughter, have to be among these highborn peers and their families?

She caught sight of the duke, but he was not the comfortable old gentleman who puttered with flowers and told stories to his granddaughter. He presented an intimidating appearance in his black superfine jacket and breeches. Even Mrs. Barrington was correct to the shade in an elegant gown of half mourning.

Panic shot through Hope, but Jonathan, not noticing, led her to a young handsome gentleman of medium height with startling blue eyes and a thick thatch of blond hair.

"David, may I make you acquainted with Hope Forrest, Celeste's companion. Hope, Viscount Waverly."

Hope trembled when the young man gently took her hand and almost fainted when he kissed it. "David Fairen, viscount Waverly, at your service, lovely lady."

Her pulses pounding, Hope stuttered, "Y. . .Yes." Which brought a smile of amusement to David's eyes and a blush to Hope's cheeks.

Taking her arm in his from the frowning Jonathan, David laughed. "Now, Jon, this ball is in our honor, is it not? Given that, I have every right to appropriate the young lady."

"I haven't introduced her around," argued Jon.

"I am quite capable of doing that." David proceeded to take her around to his parents and siblings.

"Father, Mother, may I make present Hope Forrest. Hope, Lord and Lady Thorwall."

Hope managed not to humiliate herself by her curtsy she had practiced with Celeste and Gwen before the mirror. The earl was an older version of his son and had the same startling blue eyes that his sister, the marchioness, had inherited.

Earlier that evening, Gwen (whose own eyes were a soft blue) called them "Barrington eyes" as she dreamily recounted one of the stories of her parent's courtship. "They fell in love when my mother was just a girl not much older than me. And Aunt Celeste's story is almost as wonderful." Hope could understand why the girl was so taken with her aunt.

David's mother and Celeste's namesake was still beautiful, with her thick dark hair set off by diamond stars and a figure which reminded Hope sharply of her own lack.

There was no doubt of the affection the families all held for one another, and jealousy once more welled up inside Hope, but she had no time to brood for David also introduced her around to the vicar and his wife and several neighbors. Hope was surprised to find a squire or two among them, and even more so to find them just as accepted as the peers.

When Miter announced dinner, David fended off Jonathan for the honor of escorting Hope into dinner. Somehow entering the formal dining hall on David's arm gave Hope a new appreciation for the ancient chamber with its vaulted ceiling and the monstrous fireplace on the left over which hung battle-axes, swords, and other medieval implements of war used by Glynis ancestors.

Her gaze drifted from the family coat of arms with its many quarterings over another huge fireplace at the far end, to the carefully preserved tapestries on the cold stone walls picturing the family history in tiny, realistic stitches.

The marquess took his usual place at the head of the long table, while the marchioness sat at the other end. Stiff-backed footman held the sturdy rosewood chairs with their cabriole legs for the diners, but David himself seated Hope beside him at the long refractory table. Hope glowed under his attentiveness, scarcely noticing the utensils engraved with the Glynmouth crest or the Wedgwood, gold-edged dinnerware.

Throughout the many courses, Jonathan frowned at the dazed look on Hope's face every time she turned toward his cousin. Hope's wonderment lasted until David asked, "Have I met you somewhere before? In London, mayhap?"

Hope froze and shook her head.

"I seldom forget a face, and there is something definitely familiar about yours. Hmm." At the almost desperate pain in Hope's eyes, David stopped.

Under the table he grasped her hand and squeezed it. "Forget I said anything," he whispered. His kindness brought tears to Hope's eyes which she hid behind her serviette.

The marchioness, however, had also heard the exchange and her eyes narrowed thoughtfully. What was the girl hiding? She seemed innocent enough. Was she merely a runaway, or was there more to the story? Pursing her lips, Faith determined to discover the truth of the matter once and for all. . .for her own peace of mind.

Later, Hope entered the long hall which she and Celeste, along with the staff, had decorated with gold and red streamers, flowers entwined around columns, and Greek statues brought in from the garden for the night. It was an enchanting room. When Gwen had been allowed downstairs earlier, she'd clapped her hands in awe. "It is just the right place to meet a prince."

Thankfully, Hope did not have to stand in line welcoming guests who came for the ball. As the room filled to overflowing, Jonathan found her behind a statue of King David. Holding up his quizzing glass, Jonathan pretended to study the only partially draped figure. "Don't believe this is the David you wish to spend the evening with."

Hope's embarrassment turned to anger. "You are trying to embarrass me, Jonathan."

"And succeeding," he chortled. "That was your punishment for deserting me earlier, but now I have you all to myself—and I shall take advantage of the situation."

"You are not really hurt, are you? You know I would not."

Jonathan shook his head. "Hope, you are far too serious. Of course I am jealous that I can be with you for weeks and you treat me like a brother, but one look at dear cousin David, and you melt."

Hope clapped hands over her burning cheeks. "Oh no!" Humiliated, she picked up her skirts and turned to escape.

"Wait Hope!" called Jonathan, going after her. "I never meant. Oh bother."

Scowling, David pulled him back. "I think you've done enough damage for one night, Jon. Leave Hope to me."

"It's you she prefers anyway," he muttered.

David caught up with Hope at the bottom of the stairs. Taking her arm firmly, he led her into the nearest parlour. Finding it empty, he closed the door.

"Let me go." Hope struggled to no avail.

David gave her a little shake. "Hope Forrest, listen to me. I heard what Jonathan told you."

Hope's cheeks blossomed, then paled. "Trust me, no one but Jonathan would find anything unusual in your behavior."

"And you?" Hope hung her head, unable to meet the derision in his eyes.

"I dare say you have had little chance to meet eligible men in your life. I am honored you like me."

Like you, thought Hope. *Oh my.*

"Please look at me, Hope." Slowly she raised her head. "Now I want to see a smile. I want people to know you enjoy being with me."

"Oh, I do," she burst out and felt her cheeks grow warm.

David chuckled. "That's better. Now smile and pretend, for tonight, you are the fairest of the ladies and I am your adoring knight."

"Like a dream?" asked Hope.

David bowed slightly. "As you wish my lady. Pretend you have just met your handsome prince."

Hope was sure she had. In David's arms, for the first time in her life, she truly felt beautiful. *Don't be daft,* she scolded herself firmly. *He is only playing the gallant.*

But her heart refused to listen. Did she imagine it, or did David's wonderful blue eyes darken when he released her to Jonathan and then to the other gentlemen who begged a dance. In a rare moment when both she and Celeste stood together, Celeste smiled, "Isn't this fun? I love dancing."

"And you are definitely the belle of the ball tonight," said Hope, her eyes on David who was dancing with the vicar's wife, a portly woman who nonetheless handled herself with dignity.

Celeste followed her gaze. "You've been busy yourself, though I do believe a certain cousin of mine would prefer to keep you to himself."

"Oh," Hope's cheeks reddened. "David is just being kind."

"David is that, but I think this time he is quite smitten." Celeste grinned wickedly.

"Don't jest, please," begged Hope. Somehow Celeste's teasing tarnished the preciousness of the feelings she held.

Hope's seriousness wiped the smirk from the kind-hearted girl's face. "I am sorry, Hope, if I hurt your feelings," Celeste whispered, "but. . ." She watched her cousin push through the crowd, for many more had been invited to the dance than to the dinner, "I really think David likes you. I'm glad."

David bowed. "May I have this dance, Miss Forrest?"

Hope drew back her hand. "But David, I have already danced with you twice."

"So you have, but this is a simple country affair. Surely no one will refine too much on us taking an extra turn about the floor, especially if," he quirked an eyebrow at Celeste, "my dear cousin would deem one of her many partners the honor of a third dance as well."

Laughing, Celeste pulled one of the local swains onto the floor as the band struck up a waltz. "Now then," David put his arms about Hope, holding her a trifle more closely than strictly conventional, "I shall dance with the prettiest girl here."

Hope tried to appear merely polite, "I am sure you jest, but thank you anyway."

"But you are, Hope. You are a lovely person inside and out, and I have every intention of getting better acquainted."

"Pretty?" she inquired.

David thought she sought further flowery compliments until he looked down into her pain-filled eyes. Missing a step, he stopped, took her arm, and led her from the floor. "It's a beautiful October evening. Will you walk with me in the garden?"

Hope could only nod and follow David out in the cool night air. A light breeze rippled her golden curls, and she breathed in the fragrance of the late blooming flowers and pungent herbs. "It is a wonderful night," she sighed, then blushed for it was the young man at her side who made it wonderful.

Silently David turned her to face him. A moment later his

lips softly touched hers. Hope thought her heart stopped beating, then it pounded in her chest until she thought she might faint.

"Oh, David," she breathed once he released her. "You mustn't."

A wry smile twisted his lips. "I know," he murmured, and once more captured her soft lips.

❧

As Hope went to sleep that night, dreaming of a blue-eyed, blond-haired knight, Nathaniel stumbled away from the gaming table at a house of pleasure he frequented with Beaucamp.

"Come lad," called Beaucamp, "so you are a might under the hatches. You'll recover. Come now."

Even cup shot, Nathaniel knew enough to refuse. "I am already under the hatches, as you well know, Arland. Father does not make idle threats, and I've already used my allowance for this month."

Beaucamp frowned. "Then grow up and earn it back. Sit." He grinned wickedly. "Afterward, I promise to pay for a very special reward."

Feeling trapped, Nathaniel plopped back into his chair. With a growl he picked up the cards Beaucamp dealt out to him.

Two hours later, Beaucamp held a pile of Nathaniel's IOUs, and Nathaniel sat slumped in his chair. Where in the world was he to get the money to pay his debt? Anger stirred against his friend, and not for the first time. More and more he suspected Beaucamp enjoyed leading him into debauchery. Nathaniel did not understand why Beaucamp haunted the domestic bureaus. He had not wanted to know.

Beaucamp hid his growing anxiety about locating Hope from his friend. Friend? Not exactly. But at least until he found his erstwhile heiress, he had the lad's monies. His pressing debts made it imperative he find her. . .or some equally complacent wealthy young lady. As for Nate, Beaucamp eyed him disdainfully, the lad had about served his twisted purposes.

Nate found Beaucamp staring significantly at his jade signet ring. With a sigh, Nathaniel pulled it off his finger and plunked it down on the table in front of the baron. "Security only," he muttered, "until I can repay my debt to you."

He watched Beaucamp pick up the ring with long slim fingers and slip it on. "Worth something," he said. Then getting up, he motioned for the shapely over-painted madam who hurried to his side.

"Sir Beaucamp," she all but snickered, "how can I help you?"

"Something special for my friend here, on me, of course. Mayhap he would enjoy one of your latest acquisitions." The two exchanged a knowing look.

"I have just the thing. And you, milord?"

"Where are you keeping that red-haired number you just got in?"

"I have those two girls side-by-side in some special rooms upstairs," she told him.

"What did she mean?" asked Nathaniel. "What have you to do with her girls?"

Beaucamp waved aside the questions as he followed the woman up the stairs and down the hall.

When she unlocked a door and swung it open, Nathaniel glimpsed a girl cringing in the corner. He only got a glimpse of Beaucamp's face as he entered, but it turned his stomach. Turning away, he tried to act nonchalant. "Madam. I fear I am not up to this tonight. Mayhap another evening."

Feeling her eyes on his back as he stumbled down the

stairs and out into the fresh air, Nathaniel knew she was not fooled. The snap of chill in the air cleared his head. Inside he felt empty. He had partaken of all London had to offer—the routs, the balls, the receptions. He attended dinners graced by the King and mingled with the highest of the land.

Then he met Beaucamp who introduced him to serious gambling and other, lower forms of pleasure. He took to it with all the rebellion in his heart. Now he ached. He tried to forget the look of terror and desperation on the face of that girl. Tried to pretend the girl was simply acting out a role, but in his heart he knew the truth.

The pain drove Nate to hurry his pace until, with surprise, he found himself looking up at the family's town house. Drizzle caused him to run up the stairs for shelter.

The young Miter opened the door. "Milord?"

"Wipe the shock from your face. I am cold and tired," growled the earl. "I need a drink and a bed."

Later in his bedchamber, Nate tried unsuccessfully to drown himself in the bottle.

Mayhap the people of Ravenhill were right. Mayhap there was no hope for him. . .not ever. Still, he had made a bargain with his father and he would honor that bargain. For now at least, he would return home.

For some reason, instead of filling him with anger, the thought of going home brought a strange sense of relief. Yes, it was time to go home. He thought of Gwen. Of all his family, Gwen was the only one he truly loved, the only one he would not hurt for the world. Gwen would welcome him home.

four

“Mother, please,” growled Nate, wrenching himself from his mother’s embrace.

“Nathaniel,” said his father sharply, “don’t act like that with your mother.”

A muscle in the earl’s cheek twitched. “My apologies, Mother. But I am a man grown now, not a lad to hang onto your skirts.”

Faith swallowed her disappointment. “I am glad you are home, son. Are you staying?”

Nate shrugged, ignoring the thundering scowl on the face of the marquess as he addressed his son. “How deep were you playing this time? Who gulled you into losing your money? You *are* in debt, are you not?”

On the verge of explaining the truth of the matter, Nate’s eyes narrowed at the disgust on his father’s face. “Don’t concern yourself, Father mine,” he shot back, “I shall see to my own vowels.”

The marquess snorted, “Not with Jon’s money.”

Nate swung to face him. “You will never let me forget that, will you? Never permit me to forget I am not my saintly brother Jonathan. Well, I am not Jon.” Then more quietly, “Why can’t you accept me as I am?”

He recovered quickly. “It hardly matters, does it? Who knows,” he laughed harshly, “mayhap the devil will take back his own and your wonderful Jonathan will be your heir.”

He held his father's gaze. "That's what you really want, isn't it?"

The marquess broke the gaze first, but not before seeing the hurt and disappointment in his son's eyes. Silently the marquess blasted himself, hating himself for how he felt. Looking up, he said, "Nate, I—"

"Never mind, Father. I well know I haven't been the most lovable of sons." His harsh laughter wrenched his mother's heart.

"Nathaniel," she said, holding back the hurt, "I love you, but Jesus Christ loves you so much more than ever I could. Bitterness never solved anything. Jesus can take it away. If only you would—"

"Mother, not now. I am not in the mood for one of your sermons. . .however well meant."

At that moment the door opened and Gwen ran into the room. "Nate!" she squealed, throwing herself into his arms. "You came home!"

"Just for you, Poppet," he teased, swinging her about. "So you missed your big, bad brother."

Gwen giggled. "Oh, Nate, you've never been a big bad brother to me."

Setting her down, Nathaniel stared down soberly. "And I would never hurt you, Poppet, nor allow anyone to hurt you. Not ever." He said this so fiercely, Faith smiled.

Taking his hand, Gwen tugged him toward the door. "Come on Nate, I want you to meet my new governess. You'll like her, and you will never believe how we found her."

Nate grimaced. "Now, Gwen." He searched for some plausible excuse. "Look, Poppet, I am pretty tired right now. And look at me—I am not fit to meet anyone as wonderful as this new paragon of yours." Inwardly he groaned, imaging either a hen-witted lady who had no means, or some dragon breathing fire. "I need time to bathe and dress for dinner."

Dropping his hand, Gwen surveyed her brother sternly. "Mayhap you are right. If you are going to fall in love with Miss Hope, you will have to have a turn out better than Jon's."

"Fall in love." A glint of amusement sparkled in Nate's dark eyes. "So you want me to beat his time with this Miss Hope. Not too sporting, Poppet."

Gwen answered with little girl logic. "I love Miss Hope, and I want you to love her, too."

Interested in spite of himself, Nate said, "Umm. I shall have to see why you are so enamored of the young lady."

The look on his face bothered the marquess, who cautioned. "Son, remember Miss Hope is a gently bred young lady, not one of your London flirts."

Nate only smiled, a smile of pure mischief which made his mother's heart quail.

When Nate excused himself, Faith searched the eyes of her husband. "He wouldn't really hurt Hope. . .would he?"

Catching her outstretched hand, the marquess pulled her to him. "I don't know, my darling. I don't know. I never could understand the boy, and he knows it."

In the long gallery, Jonathan took Hope's arm. "Now this is a portrait of the second duke of Glynmouth, and this of his lovely wife."

Interested, Hope said, "She is dark, like your aunt. Was the duchess also from Spain?"

"No, she was a princess, a minor princess, from Italy. He was quite the traveler—the ancestor who brought back many of the Greek and Italian statues and vases. He also managed to firmly entrench the family coffers. So far, every duke since has increased our holdings. So far," he muttered darkly, thinking of his brother.

As though reading his mind, Hope asked, "About your brother?"

Startled, Jonathan stared at her. "Don't tell me you have mother's gift of practically reading minds?"

"I thought your mother and father only did that to each other."

"Father, yes, but mother has a frightening habit of picking up on just what one is thinking. . .or planning." He grinned, "Made childhood mischief very difficult. Now if you have the same gift. . ."

"I *wish* I could read minds," laughed Hope ruefully, "but you are perfectly safe with me."

Raising an eyebrow, Jon stared down into her upturned face. "Don't you know I am a dangerous man? Why any minute now I just might pull you into my arms and kiss you breathless."

Laughing, Hope pulled away from him, "I think I am safe enough with you."

Jon's face darkened momentarily. "You think so." For a moment he grasped her arms but released her when the laughter on her face faded into fear. "My apologies, Hope." He smiled to reassure her. "You are simply too lovely for this poor country lad."

As he hoped, she giggled. "Country lad indeed. Aren't you heir to a dukedom?"

This took Jonathan back. "Why, no. My twin was born first. I fear, if you set your sites on this lad, you'll find I have but a small trust fund. . .thanks to that self-same brother. . .and will inherit but a hunting box in Scotland."

"But you love Ravenhill," Hope burst out. "I know how hard you work."

This brought a smile to Jon's lips. "Now there's a woman after my own heart, a woman who will fight for me."

"Isn't it difficult to work so hard, knowing your brother will inherit?" she asked curiously, then caught herself. "Oh, dear, I am sorry for being so inquisitive. I just know how much my father loved his estate even though it had not been in our family for generations. He purchased it from a peer who had to sell the place in order to pay his gambling debts."

Jon sobered. "So you are not willing to marry the younger son?"

Facing him, Hope shot back, "If I loved someone, I would not care if he were a chimney sweep. Wealth or land or family holdings have *nothing* to do with love. And don't you forget that, Jonathan Fairen. If that's all I wanted, I would be married by now." Tears sparkled in her eyes and she turned away, but Jon held her arms.

"Look. Now it is my turn to apologize. You know how I tease."

"Oh, there you are," called Celeste, walking toward them in an afternoon gown of soft green. "Hope, Gwen is asking for you. She's in a dither about you meeting Nate."

Jon swung about abruptly. "Nate, you say?"

"He's come," said Celeste, linking her arm with Hope's. Her eyes twinkled. "I do believe she intends that you have some competition for Hope's favor, brother."

With a grimace, Jon excused himself. As he hurried from the gallery, Celeste whispered, "Course, I know neither one has a chance against cousin David."

Hope flushed. "Oh, Celeste! Obviously he didn't feel the

same way. I haven't seen him since the ball."

"I thought you knew. He volunteered to go to Bearwood Hall to bring home a couple of mares father is acquiring from the duke St. Clair, along with several old masterpieces. I heard father say that since St. Clair is determined to sell off family treasures, at least he can make certain they stay in the family."

"A relative, the duke St. Clair?"

"They are distantly related. Let's see if I can remember how. The fourth duke is the grandnephew of my grandmother. Though, from what I hear, the duke isn't so grand. Doing his best to decimate the family coffers, along with that promiscuous wife of his," she added scathingly.

Hope blushed. "Celeste, please. That is not a subject for a young lady to discuss."

Immediately contrite, Celeste sighed, "I know, but it makes me so angry. You just don't know. The duke and his family made his younger brother the dupe in something awful which happened and made him go away."

"And you liked this younger son?"

"He liked visiting Ravenhill, and I think he was not too happy at home. He was both kind and fun. We all thought of him as, well, like one of the family." Her face darkened, "Then he had to go away."

"What happened to him?"

She shrugged. "I don't know. As far as I know, no one has heard from him for a couple years."

Reaching their rooms, Gwen pounced on Hope. "Miss Hope, the most wonderful thing happened. Nate came home and now you can meet him. He is the best brother ever, and I want him to love you as much as I do."

"Oh, Gwen, I am sure your brother is very nice, but—"

"No he isn't," interrupted Celeste. "He is mean and irresponsible."

"He is not!" shrieked Gwen. "He is kind and he loves me."

"That's true enough," Celeste admitted. "But no one else likes him much. And you know how he hurt Mother by running off to London."

"Father let him go."

"After he threatened to run away. That's the way he handles everything. When things get tough, he runs away."

Her words smote Hope, who stumbled across to the window. Outside, thin clouds stretched across the blue sky. Tree branches, with leaves beginning to turn orange and brown, fluttered in the rising wind.

How Hope wanted to forget those words and more—the contempt with which they were spoken. She too ran away, but she had no other choice. Her lips tightened with determination. She had no other choice, being too young to fight a mother bent on marrying her off to Beaucamp. Hope stilled a shudder as the memory of that last evening flashed across her mind.

Still, Celeste's words burned in Hope's heart. She had run away. . .and kept running. Guilt tore at her heart. To own the truth, she had not felt peace since leaving home.

Lord, I could not stay, not after that, she defended. *You know I could not stay.*

Again she heard the quiet inner voice: *Why could you not trust Me to take care of you?*

"Miss Hope."

Pasting on a smile, Hope met Gwen's questioning face. "My apologies. What did you say?"

"Tonight, will you wear the gown you wore to the ball?"

Quelling a grin, Hope shook her head, "Your brother would think me a regular pea-goose if I flaunted such a gown for a family meal. You wouldn't want that, would you?"

"No. No, of course not."

Hope edged the girls from her room. "Then will you trust me to wear proper attire?"

"Of course I trust you, Miss Hope. You always do what's right."

Shutting the door, Hope leaned against it. Gwen's innocent declaration hit home. Always do what was right? Reaching for the bell cord, she gave it a violent tug. If only she could put her past where it belong. . .in the past. But as long as she paraded as Hope Forrest, Hope knew her past would never be settled, never be forgotten. And there was the matter of her inheritance.

As was his wont, Jonathan showed up to escort her to dinner. Gowned in the deceptively simple gown of amaranthus with its white sash and matching pinkish purple ribbons to hold up her natural golden curls, Hope smiled at the admiration in his eyes.

"My lady." He held out his arm. "Such an attractive picture you make with all that golden hair."

Wholly in charity with one another, Jonathan escorted her to the anteroom, where the family gathered for dinner.

Downstairs, Celeste presented her brother Nate, whose eyes widened at the girl on his brother's arm. Knowing his brother as well as he did, Nate recognized the signs of infatuation. Raising his quizzing glass, he surveyed the young woman. *Would take two large hands to span that waist,* he thought unkindly, continuing his perusal. True her shoulders were a trifle wide for her height and she had none of the London polish he preferred, nor the figure, yet she looked like she would make a comfortable armful.

"Hope, may I make you known to my brother Nathaniel, earl of Glynis. Nate, Miss Hope Forrest, my companion and friend."

"I thought this lovely lady was a lowly governess."

"I am that, too, milord," acknowledged Hope with a curtsey.

Smiling his most devastating smile, Nate bowed over her hand, holding it a fraction longer than convention dictated. Blushing, Hope pulled her hand free and turned to find Jonathan scowling.

"She won't fall for your seductive tricks, brother," Jonathan told him stiffly.

Nate's eyelid drooped languidly. "Jealous, brother?"

Hope found the older twin delighted in baiting his brother. Dinner became a nightmare, with the young men vying for her attentions. Had she the bronze of a town season she would have known how to take their flattery with a laugh and a wave of her fan. As it was, their rivalry depressed her.

In the parlour after dinner, Hope sat down in a dusky rose, wingbacked chair, missing the comforting presence of Emily who had been invited to spend some time at Thorn Hall. But Nate had no intention of letting her off so easily. Well into his game, he daringly took her hand and pulled her to her feet.

"Not good to lounge about after a meal. The wind has died down and 'tis a lovely night for a walk in the rose garden."

Hope protested. "It is still chill outside at this time of night."

"Not a problem, fair lady." Nate merely commanded a

maid to fetch a wrap. "There," he said, brazenly placing the wrap about her shoulders.

"We cannot leave Celeste," Hope said.

Nate frowned. "She doesn't want to go with us."

At the plea in Hope's eyes, Celeste gracefully got to her feet. "La, I do believe a turn in the garden would help me sleep better."

Nate was not in the least pleased to wait while a maid fetched a wrap for his sister, but Hope refused to budge without her.

Much to the amusement of his parents, Jonathan got to his feet. "Umm. I do believe I also need to stretch my legs."

At Nate's thundering scowl, Celeste chortled, "La, definitely a turn."

The three moved through the velvet curtains at the large french windows and onto a patio leading down the steps to the flagged path of the formal rose garden. Arrogantly, Nate took Hope's hand, and she was hard put to free herself.

Noting her struggle, Jonathan stepped between them, tucking her hand in his arm.

"Celeste needs an escort," he calmly told his fuming brother. Behind them, Hope heard Nate. "Here, sis," he growled, "let me take your arm."

"I don't like your attitude by half," Celeste told him, moving away.

"Botheration, Celeste. Surely you don't expect fulsome compliments. You're my sister, not a lady."

Jonathan chuckled, "That will put her in a taking, brother mine. Not a lady?"

Churlishly, Nate grabbed her arm. "You know what I meant."

Not wanting to cause further trouble, Celeste kept her retort to herself. Hope sensed her frustration and tried to include her. “Look at the sky. All those stars. They’re like points of light on black velvet.”

Jonathan followed her gaze. “I see what you mean.”

Dropping Celeste’s arm, Nate moved up to stand beside Hope. “Not near as handsome as the lady at my side,” he said smoothly.

Celeste sniggered, while Jonathan struggled for a compliment. “You are as pretty as the heavens,” he blurted.

This time Nate snickered. “Now that will turn a lady’s head. Comes from burying yourself in the country with nothing but farmer’s wives for company.”

“Oh, stop it,” cried Hope, “Stop it, you two. I am sick and tired of your bickering over me. Argue if you must, but leave me out of it.”

With that, she took Celeste’s arm and ushered the surprised younger girl back the way they had come.

“Now see what you’ve done,” said Jon.

A smile played around Nate’s sensuous lips. “The chit is a continual surprise. Where did you find her?”

Finding it, as always, difficult to stay angry at his brother for long, Jon regaled him with the tale of Hope’s introduction to the household.

“Are you saying no one knows where she came from or who she is?”

“I suppose Mother knows—you know how she is about these things—and father since she tells him everything, but all the rest of us know is her name. Gwen has some silly notion the girl is a runaway princess or some such fiddle-faddle. You know how she is.”

“Gwen is all right. Leave her be. Now about the girl. Have you no idea who she might be?”

"Only that David thought he recognized her at first, but she denied ever meeting him. And," he added dryly, "she would have remembered."

"So the girl has a tendre for our cousin, does she?" Winning the girl was becoming more of a challenge all the time.

In the parlour, Hope and Celeste excused themselves and went up to their rooms. Celeste detested sleeping in what she termed the nursery, so she had rooms on the floor below, but Hope found her bedchamber warm, welcoming, and comfortable. Besides, as Gwen's governess she felt it imperative to be near her charge.

When Hope went to check on the girl, she found her awake, her eyes dancing with excitement. "Did you meet Nate? Did you like him? Isn't he handsome?" the girl rattled on.

Once Gwen stopped to take a breath, Hope told her, "I did meet him, and of course, he is handsome. He looks just like Jonathan."

"But did you like him?"

"You have to give me more time to get to know him," Hope said, not wanting to hurt the little girl's feelings. "Now, lie down, and I'll tuck you in."

Later in her own room, Hope relaxed under Jenny's impersonal ministrations. When she finally slipped into bed, Hope stared into the darkness. "Lord, I am so tired. Please help me know how to deal with Nate and Jonathan. I know they aren't truly serious about me. Mayhap that makes it hurt all the more, but I don't want to hurt Jonathan."

Hope wondered if God even heard her prayer. Then again, she hadn't been listening to Him very well. Her heart cried out for the absent David, even as she castigated herself for reading anything serious into his attentions that unforgettable night of the ball.

❧

The next week was anything but pleasant. Jonathan and Nate continually sought Hope out to ply her with flattery and other flummery as though she were a London belle. When she rode, Jonathan rode alongside, cutting out any of her attempts to converse with Celeste. Nate was worse, for he invariably interrupted her lessons with Gwen, much to the little girl's delight and Hope's frustration.

Part of her relished the persistent attentions of her two suitors, for they made her feel desirable. But the practical side of her nature kept her feet firmly planted on the truth about herself. She was not a desirable woman. If one of her sisters suddenly walked into the room, Hope well knew neither twin would spare her a second glance.

One afternoon she took Gwen to see the girl's grandfather, hoping for a respite, but the young men found her even there. Amused, the duke watched the sometimes heated rivalry of his grandsons before sending them on their way. He waved away Hope's profuse thanks with a laugh. "Always the same with a pretty girl." Hope blushed under his wink.

In the evenings, both brothers escorted her to dinner and both sought a seat next to her at the table. Feeling Nate's knee against hers, Hope moved away only to encounter Jonathan, whose eyes danced with delight. Silly, perhaps, but she felt trapped. If only David would return.

She blushed. While his gentle kisses still burned on her lips, by now David had probably forgotten all about her. The thought was humbling and quite put her out of countenance with the twins.

Worn out from her constant efforts to avoid the two brothers, especially Nate with his overfamiliar hands, Hope also lost her appetite.

"Enough, Nate, Jon," commanded the marquess. "Leave Miss Forrest alone. From now on you two will sit on the other side of the table. Is that clear?" Hope's tremulous smile of gratitude confirmed the marquess's suspicions that the marked attentions discomfited her. He smiled in return. Too bad they did not know more about her. She might well be just what Nate needed to settle him down.

Hope would have been horrified had she even suspected the marquess's train of thought. After dinner she excused herself early and escaped to her room. Gwen came running out, her nightshirt flapping at her heels. "Hope, why aren't you down with Nate?"

Unable to deal with the little girl's chatter, Hope distracted Gwen with a story, then tucked her firmly into bed. But unable to sleep herself, Hope sat on the large rug in front of the fire. The October day had turned chilly, and Hope was glad for the warmth of the fire. She read until late, then began combing out her hair which had grown out since her arrival.

Mesmerized by the crackle of the roaring fire, Hope did not hear the door open, nor the footsteps until he overshadowed her. Startled she glanced up. "Nate, what are you doing here? Gwen is asleep, and it is too late to awaken her."

"I did not come to see Gwen," Nate told her, taking in her dishevelment with obvious interest. "In fact I fully intend she get her rest."

Hope's heart thudded against her tight chest. "Then I think you'd better leave," she said, getting to her feet with as much dignity as she could manage.

"Playing the fine lady, are we?" Nate murmured softly. "Mother may treat you like family, but you are only a governess, only hired help."

"And they're fair game, is that it?" asked Hope, her voice rising.

"Umm." Nate ran his fingers lightly through her hair, glowing red-gold in the firelight. "A passionate woman, I think," he said, pulling her close.

"Your jest has gone far enough, Nate. Now, let me go."

"I think not, Hope Forrest. . .if that is your real name. I think we will deal quite well together."

"If you think I'll marry you. . ."

"Marry?" laughed Nate softly. "The heir to a dukedom does not marry a nobody."

"Then why are you here?" Staring up into his eyes, Hope saw the same look she had seen from Beaucamp and shuddered.

"Lord, help me," she cried. "Please, help me!"

"Nate," came a sleepy voice from the doorway, "what are you doing here? Did you come to see me?" Gwen's face brightened.

"Ah," Nate angrily muttered under his breath before turning to face the young girl with a sheepish grin. "That I did, Poppet."

"Papa will be angry you got me up, but I'm glad."

Recovering her composure with some difficulty, Hope said firmly. "Gwen must go to bed."

Instead of leaving, Nate took the girl's hand. "Come, Poppet. Miss Hope is right. I should not have disturbed you. Now hop into bed."

Taking advantage of the distraction, Hope slipped off to her room and locked the door. Later the handle turned, then stopped. Nate laughed softly. "Next time, my girl, I shall see we are not interrupted."

There would be no next time. The next morning before dawn, Hope, wrapped in a warm cloak and wearing sturdy ankle boots, sneaked down the back staircase and out a side door. This time she left a letter saying good-bye, without explaining the truth of the matter or exposing the earl. She hated him as she hated Beaucamp, for destroying her chance of happiness, her chance for a home and security and love. Forlornly, she wondered if David would ever think of her once she was gone.

At least this time she had some place to go—once she found the posting inn from which she could catch a stage. She was thankful she had written Harry's sister, telling her about his last hours. She slapped her pocket. Yes, she had not forgotten the letter de Court's sister had written in return, inviting Hope to come to London.

For hours, Hope walked. The sun rose warm, but a chilly wind caused her to pull the wool cape more closely about her shoulders. More time passed, still she trod on. Her stomach growled; she felt a blister start on her heel. Was this all to be a repeat of her escape from home?

The sun was high in the sky, and still she walked. The air grew colder, the wind rose, but still she plodded on. Disgruntled, Hope began to question her reasons for running away. Surely the marchioness would not permit Nate to harm her, that is, if she believed Hope. From the things Celeste told her, Hope realized the foolishness of her action. The Glynises were a far cry from her own manipulative mother. Once more, she had made the wrong decision.

"Lord, I'll go back. I will tell them about Nate." Facing back the way she had come, Hope set her feet toward Ravenhill, the brown grass crunching under her boots. After an hour of walking, she was not so sure. Nothing looked familiar. Frequently Hope stopped to get her bearings. The sky had darkened, and often dark clouds obscured the sun, chilling the air.

Frightened, Hope tried a different direction, then another.She blinked back tears and warmed her hands with her breath which steamed in the air. Finally she admitted the truth: she was truly and thoroughly lost.

The sun began to descend into the west when Hope tripped over a fallen branch and fell. With a cry, she crashed to the browning pasture grass at the bottom of a rise. Dazed, Hope sat up.

To one side ran a path through a thick wood. On the other a stone fence rose in the air. Listening for sounds of life, Hope only heard the gurgle and rush of a nearby river, the cry of a jay overhead, and the scuffle of a small animal in the brush.

Gingerly, Hope wiggled her ankle, then cried out at the pain. With a mighty heave, she sought to move the heavy branch, but screamed as it bit farther into her leg. She tried reaching down to scratch away the sod about her ankle, but her foot was twisted in a fork of the branch and no amount of digging would free her. She needed the thing moved, and she was not in a position to do so. Wiping her dirty hands on her cloak, Hope shivered on the cold hard ground.

"Help! Help someone!" she yelled. "Help!"

Her voice echoed back, "Help!" No one heard. No one came.

Again she yelled, louder this time. "Help someone. I need help. My leg is caught." Again no one heard and no one came to her rescue.

Trying to find a more comfortable position, Hope lay back to rest. After a day of walking with no nourishment, Hope was exhausted and discouraged. Angrily she wiped tears from her cheeks with her grubby hands, making mud tracks down her face. Clenching her teeth, she determined to stop the tears, but this time determination was not enough.

Closing her eyes, Hope let them fall.

"Please Lord, help me. What am I to do? Every time I try to save myself, I get in a mess. All I need now is rain. Ow!" Her hand covered her cheeks. They were stinging from sharp cold. The stinging cold stabbed her again, then shot down like tiny arrows.

"Not snow, Lord. Hail more like," she muttered, pulling the cape about her head for protection.

Once night fell, Hope knew her chances of survival were slim. Once more she screamed, "Help! Oh, help somebody!" Listening intently, she heard only the whining wind.

Covering her face, she wept as she had not wept since the death of her father. "Why don't you save me, God?" she accused.

Pictures flashed in her mind. The timely rescue of de Court and his courtly protection, the "coincidence" of Mrs. Haskle stopping along the road and her rescue. Again the "coincidence" of running into Mrs. Barrington. Suddenly she realized coincidence had nothing to do with it. Despite her disobedience in running away, God had still had His hand of protection upon her.

Gently He continued calling her back to Himself. Broken now, Hope bowed her head. "Forgive me, Lord. Forgive me for not trusting You. I ran because I was afraid, but I keep running. Running away is not an answer, is it? All it gets me is more trouble." She sucked in more cold air.

"At least Beaucamp offered marriage. I am tired of running my own life, Lord. I am not very good at it. Forgive me, Lord Jesus. Help me trust You for the desire of my heart to be safe. . .and loved.

"Help me get out of this mess I've gotten myself into, Jesus. I'll do whatever You want me to. But. . .but if You want me to come home to You, that's all right, too." Hope continued to pray until peace poured over her, warming her as a fire never could.

So intense was her communion, Hope almost missed the faint cry, “Hope. Hope. Where are you, Hope?”

Sitting up, Hope screamed with all her might. “Here! I am here. I am here.”

“I hear you. Keep calling.”

Excited, Hope needed no urging. “I am here. Here!”

She stared up into the flaying snow, “Lord, no one can find me here. Please help him find me.” Just as suddenly as it had begun, the icy snow stopped, and the wind died to a murmur.

Through the growing gloom of darkness appeared a ghostly figure. Hope gasped. “David!”

five

"Hope!" strong arms held her close, causing her heart to quicken. "I thought we'd never find you." Stripping off his heavy cape, David wrapped it about the shivering young woman. "Now, what's the problem?"

"My leg," Hope said. "I fell and caught it in this branch. Silly thing to do." She grimaced as David put a hand on the tree branch.

Only half seeing in the darkness, David groped for her ankle, felt the position of it in the branch. He tried raising the limb, only to have Hope cry out as it wrenched her ankle. "You are truly stuck, Hope." After surveying the problem as best he could in the light available, David snapped off several smaller branches and dropped them near Hope. A moment later he strode off into the night.

"David," cried Hope, panic rising. "Where are you?"

She jumped when he spoke close to her ear. "I am right here, Hope. I just went to the fence to find a couple of large chunks from that fence. I've noticed before it needed mending."

"Oh." Hope was glad he could not see her blush.

"Now, you will probably feel a tug on your ankle. Let me know if I force it too much."

Biting her lip, Hope forced herself to silence as the branch creaked and rose slightly. "What are you doing?"

"Umm. I am using those branches I broke off and the stones to tip the body of the branch up a little more. I think then I'll be able to free your ankle."

"I tried digging out. It didn't work." Hope needed the security of David's voice.

"Wrong angle," David grunted, still working to turn the thick branch. "There, got it. Now." David put his weight against the fork holding her ankle. With a loud crack it broke under his weight, flinging her leg free.

Hope yelped as her ankle crashed down against the rough bark. Then gentle hands raised it and settled it on the hard ground. "Can you move it?"

"Yes," winced Hope.

"That's good at least. It is swollen, and I have to get you home where it can be properly taken care of."

Hope bit back a cry of pain and surprise when David lifted her handily and strode toward the trees. Clutching him, Hope gasped, "Where are we going?"

David didn't answer. A moment or two later, she heard the snort of a horse and felt a cold wet nose in her face. Laughing David twisted to push the horse's head away. "Big Red likes you almost as much as I do."

Hope scarcely had time to assimilate his statement when he hoisted her sideways onto the front of his saddle, untied his horse, and swung on behind her. Putting his arms about her, he picked up the reins and headed the horse out into the rising wind toward the fence.

"You can't jump it in this weather."

She felt his warm breath against her ear. "I'm not ready for Bedlam yet. Even if I was that loose of a screw, I would not so endanger my horse."

Hope flushed. David must have felt the sudden warmth of her cheeks. "I already opened the gate next to it so we'll be perfectly safe. We'll be home before you know it. Now lean back."

The thud of her ankle against the horse made Hope shudder, and she leaned back, trying to find a more comfortable place for her legs which dangled on the left side of the large, heavily muscled animal. She felt the bunch of his shoulder muscles and yelped as the beast jumped. Beneath her, she glimpsed a ribbon of silver.

Big Red landed smoothly, but on impact, Hope's ankle throbbed. At her half sob, David drew her more closely into his arms. "It won't be long now, my Hope."

Hope, snuggled closely against her rescuer, glanced up to find him peering in the darkness, his face grim. Snow had begun falling again, its cold flakes covering them and making the large horse snort. "Are we lost?" she asked, and repeated her question when David bent his head to her lips.

He shook his head. "Big Red knows the way. I trust he'll bring us safely home."

Guilt tore at Hope's heart. But for her, the valiant horse would be safely in his stall munching hay and David would be warm and secure at Thorn Hall. "I'm sorry," she cried quietly. "I'm sorry."

Steadily, the game animal plunged through the sheeting snow. How quickly the whiteness gathered on the ground. Worried, Hope tensed, waiting for a misstep, but none came. Exhaustion overcame her, and, much to David's relief, Hope fell asleep.

"Lord," he said quietly, "please let me get her home safely." He smiled softly at the warmth of the young woman who snuggled so naturally in his arms.

❧

Hope awoke in a large bedchamber warmed by a crackling, snapping fire in the hearth of a tall fireplace. Drowsily, she gazed about the room. Two thick bedchamber candles sat on a table beside a deep cushioned chair near the bed. A dark-haired woman lay asleep against the back of the chair.

"Lady Thorwall," gasped Hope.

The woman stirred, opened her eyes, and smiled. "Hope—Miss Forrest—you are awake."

"What are you. . .I mean, where am I?"

"Thorn Hall." Again Celeste smiled, "Because it was closer. You gave us quite a scare, young lady."

Hope flushed and lowered her eyes. "I. . .I'm sorry, but. . ."

Leaning over her, Celeste pulled the covers more firmly about her shoulders, much like Hope did for Gwen. The gesture brought tears to her eyes. She never recalled her mother ever lowering herself to such a display of affection.

Ignoring the tears shimmering in the girl's eyes, Celeste explained, "We shall talk further about that in the morning if you wish. Now I want to know if you are up to eating something."

"But it must be very late," protested Hope.

"Very," agreed Lady Thorwall, "but if my information is correct, you haven't eaten in probably twenty-four hours. Correct?"

"I'm afraid so."

"I had a cold collation prepared for you. David insisted there be something ready for you just in case you awoke before morning. Now sit up, and I'll give you the tray."

Struggling to sit up, Hope groaned from the pain that shot through her ankle. As Celeste placed the tray before her and poured out some lemon juice from a nearby pitcher, Hope asked her, "How is my ankle?"

"Pretty swollen, but don't worry. It is only sprained, not broken."

"Surely a doctor didn't come out in this weather."

"No, but my duenna has had some experience in such things."

"Your duenna?" asked Hope, eagerly tackling the cold meats and cheeses.

"Like. . .a lady's maid. She came to England with me and refused to leave me even after I found Edmund."

Soothingly, Celeste talked as Hope ate. Taking the near empty tray, she put it aside and helped Hope settle back down under the covers. Blowing out the candles, she smiled. "Now that I know you are all right, I'll leave you to rest. If you need anything, ring. I put the cord beside you on your pillow there."

As she reached the door, Hope rose up on her elbows. "What about the marquess and the marchioness? Do they know I am all right?"

"Yes, David rode over and told them you were here."

"Is he all right?"

Lady Thorwall smiled at the concern in the girl's voice. "He returned over an hour ago. Don't worry. Everything will be fine. Goodnight, Hope." Softly, she closed the door behind her.

Hope closed her eyes against the pain, more in her heart than in her leg. David had risked his life because of her escapade. She would never have forgiven herself if something had happened to him. No, everything was not fine, and Hope wasn't sure if it ever would be again.

On that glum thought, Hope fell asleep.

Awaking to a room lit with candles and the glowing fire, Hope wondered if she had slept away a whole day. Sitting up, she was happy to note the pain in her ankle had lessened somewhat. Needing to tend to her personal needs, Hope threw back the covers and gingerly put her tightly wrapped foot onto the smooth wide steps against the high bed.

Sliding all the way out of bed onto her good foot, Hope held onto the bed as she tried to shift her weight to her swollen ankle in order to climb down the stairs. Pain shot up her leg, and Hope grabbed for the bed, missed, and fell off the steps to the hardwood floor.

"Miss," shrieked a maid coming into the room. Hurriedly setting down the delftware pitcher of warm water in her hands, she rushed to the fallen girl.

"Miss, are you all right?"

Groaning, Hope permitted the matronly woman to help her to her feet. Hope sat down on the steps, wincing. "I need to use. . . ."

Understanding, the woman looped Hope's arm over her shoulder and assisted her to the water closet. Not long thereafter, she assisted Hope back to her bed which now had fresh clean sheets smelling of roses. With the woman's able, no nonsense assistance, Hope washed up and was soon feeling quite the thing in a fresh nightgown of silk with dainty needlepoint around the yoked neckline.

Lady Thorwall met the maid carrying Hope's breakfast tray from the room. "Well, how's our invalid today?" she asked Hope cheerily.

"Much better, thank you. I am sorry I put everyone out so."

Celeste restrained her curiosity. "Thank God that David found you."

Hope nodded. "I should explain. . . ."

"If you wish to explain, I suggest you do so to David. He wonders why you would go off like that." She paused, "Are you up to seeing David? He's waiting outside."

"I'd like to see Lord Waverly, if it isn't too much trouble."

The sudden light in the girl's eyes gave Lady Thorwall pause. Opening the door for her son, Celeste instructed him, "Now don't tire her out."

David grinned at the sight of Hope propped up in bed, looking like a child waiting for a scold. "How's the ankle?"

"Sore." Hope drank in the sight of David in his well-fitting, rust riding jacket, breeches, and polished Hessians.

"Serves you right for going off without telling anyone."

"But I left a letter," she protested.

"Is that how you kept your promise to Lady Aven? I'll have you know, young lady," David said, pulling up a chair, turning it around, and straddling it, "that little Gwen first found your letter. She wanted to speak with you, but you had already gone. She took the letter to her sister who in turn took it to her mother. Have you any idea of the hurt you caused her ladyship or of Gwen's sense of betrayal?"

His quiet scold cast her into the dismals. Miserable, Hope blinked back tears which came so easily these days. "You don't understand."

"You are right about that. What kind of loose screw would take off without having any idea how to get to the nearest village or posting inn?"

"Was it far?" He had aroused her curiosity.

"Hope, you were not even heading in the right direction. And I thought you different from the usual selfish simpering miss. Going off from those who care about you. . .from *me.*"

Loss of his good opinion was too much, and Hope began to cry in earnest. "I'm sorry, D. . .David, but at the time it was the only thing I could think of doing."

"But why? What had the Fairens done to make you turn against them?"

Closing her eyes, Hope turned away. "Look at me, Hope. Whatever it is, you can trust me. What happened?"

Sniffing, Hope tried to stem the tears. She smiled thinly when David silently handed her his kerchief.

"Now wipe those tears." He waited while she regained her composure.

"It was Nate," she murmured, her cheeks flushing at the memory of his unexpected visit.

David stiffened. "Nate. What did he do? Was he overfamiliar?"

"He was always that," Hope sputtered angrily, "but when he came upstairs and accosted me after I had retired—"

"He what!"

Quickly Hope summed up the incident, ending, "If Gwen had not awakened—"

"The bounder! How dare he!"

Looking at David directly, Hope witnessed the fury in his eyes. "You believe me? Do you understand why I felt I must leave? It was almost like the other time."

Reaching for her hand, David crushed it in his. "Of course I believe you. And what is this about another time?"

Biting her lip, Hope knew it was time for the truth, the whole truth. "David, I have a confession. My name is not Hope Forrest; it is Hope Forrester."

"Forrester. Forrester. Somewhere I have heard that name."

"My sisters had their season, and my mother, Mrs. Forrester, often spends time in London."

"I see. I take it you ran away from home. Want to tell me why?"

Sucking in a deep breath, Hope told him about her mother's plans for her with the debauched neighbor. She told him how she saw no other way to stop the marriage other than running away from the lecher interested only in her inheritance.

"So I ran and kept running." Eyes pleading, she asked, "Now what am I to do? You know who I am. Are you going to give me over to my mother?"

David shook his head. "No, my Hope, in good conscience, I could not do such a beastly thing, but something must be done. After all, you are vastly underage."

"Twenty-one is such a long way away," she sighed. "Long before that, mother will have me married to that horrid man."

"There has to be another answer."

Yes, her heart told her, *yes. Marriage was the only answer, marriage to the man who now tightly held her hand.* Blushing at her thoughts, Hope stared at the bedcovers. "Do. . .do you think they will want me back at Ravenhill?"

"Of course they do. Gwen is wild without you. Both Nate," he frowned, "and Jon as well as the marquess were out looking for you."

"And you. How—"

"Jon rode over, neck for nothing, to recruit father and me for the search. He is in a case over you," he smiled languidly, "and he isn't the only one."

His silent perusal brought a blush to her cheeks. When she tried to turn away, he put his long slender fingers beneath her chin and forced her to look at him. "Have you feelings for Jonathan? You must tell me if you do."

"No, no," she hastened to assure him. "I care about him, yes, but only because he is like the brother I never had."

"Umm. I am glad." His boyish grin twisted her insides, and her breath came out in gasps.

Breaking away from his almost hypnotic gaze, Hope sobered. "But what about Nate? What can I do about him?"

"You leave him to me," said David grimly.

"When do I leave?" asked Hope with reluctance.

David chuckled, "From the looks of things, not for several days. It has still not stopped snowing."

"That's why it is so dark today. I thought I'd slept the whole day away." Her chortle turned into a yawn.

At Hope's embarrassed look, David chuckled. "Oh, dear, I fear mother will be out of countenance with me for tiring you." Getting up, he replaced his chair. Then leaning over, he placed a gentle kiss on Hope's forehead. "Sleep now, my Hope, and. . . ." he paused, then continued with the hint of a grin. "Dream of me."

Hope didn't need to be told. When she awoke sometime later, she found Emily sitting close by, busily knitting. "Mrs. Barrington?"

"You're awake. Hungry, too, I reckon, since you've all but slept the day away." Laying aside her knitting, Emily pulled the bell cord. "We'll see about getting you something. Now do you need anything?"

Embarrassed, Hope allowed the strong, competent woman to assist her with her personal needs. This time, though, Hope refused to return to the bed, sitting down instead in the divan by the roaring fireplace. The heat felt good on her face.

Before long, the matronly maid assigned to her brought up a tray which she set up on a table pulled up in front of Hope. Hope surveyed with dismay the tray loaded with sausages, ham, large greenhouse peaches, and a selection of cheeses, along with a pot of coffee.

"I can't begin to eat all this," she exclaimed.

"Stuff and nonsense, child," Emily sat down and picked up her knitting again. "You've lost weight since I left Ravenhill. What have you been doing to yourself?"

Forking up a sausage, Hope managed not to answer the question. She ate to the click-click of knitting needles. Hope was comforted by Emily's presence, feeling she could be more herself with the older woman than anyone else except David.

After one more bite of cheese, one more sip of the deliciously hot coffee, Emily commented, "There, that's the way to eat."

Groaning, Hope stared down at the tray, now nearly empty. "I can't believe it."

"Starving yourself never helped anything," Emily commented dryly. "Too many young things try to starve themselves into being fashionable instead of making the most of the figure God gave them."

"But I didn't. . . ," began Hope, then stopped. Her wrangle with Nate didn't need to be spread any farther.

"No matter," said Emily. "I am probably off the mark in any case. Always did think you too sensible for such fiddle-faddle.Not that going off into a snowstorm is sensible, but strong-minded people tend to do what they're going to do, just like my Jeremiah." She sighed. "He was so determined to go off to war, and off he went. Not even his mother, and certainly not I, could talk some sense into him. Thankfully, Lord Thorwall's father was with us then." Again she sighed and fell silent, her thoughts far away. "I do miss him so."

"And with your son's inheriting, you feel at loose ends." For the first time in a long time, Hope began to see beyond her own troubles to the hurts of someone else.

Emily started, her needles silent. "Why, yes. Yes, that's it exactly. I am an old woman," she confided. "They don't think I know, but I'm afraid I irritated Lord and Lady Aven to distraction. I didn't mean to interfere, but—"

"You are used to running things. As used to running things

as I am running away." A look of understanding passed between the two women.

"Running away never solved anything, child. You must meet problems head on."

"I know that now. God finally got through to me out there in the sleet and cold."

"Then something good has come out of all this."

Biting her lip, Hope wondered if she should speak her mind. "Mrs. Barrington, if you will excuse my forwardness . . . ."

"What is it, child?" the needles had begun their click-click again.

"I think you are running away, too. Running away from the pain of your husband's death," Hope empathized. "It may not be quite the same, but I lost my father scarcely a year past. I loved him very much. It was only after he died that mother. . ."

Reaching out, Emily patted her hand. "You are a courageous young woman, my dear. And you are right." She mused, "I never thought about it like that before. We have both been running, haven't we? I must think on this. Mayhap it is time I return to Ravenhill for a time, and then home."

Soon after, Emily assisted Hope to her bed. The gratitude on her face made Hope's heart soar. "Thank You, Lord," she whispered. "Thank You for letting me help her." With that, her eyes closed and she once more slept.

❧

The next few days passed pleasantly enough, with David spending much time with Hope. They grew close as they prayed together, shared together, played chess and whist together. Often Emily and Lady Thorwall found them convulsed in laughter. In those few days Hope became painfully aware that David was much more than a friend. She also determined to stop running away. The first step would be to return to Ravenhill and face Nate.

"Have you run mad," David growled, "to return to Ravenhill without telling the marquess what sent you running in the first place?"

Hope's lips tightened. "I have to face my own problems."

"Face them, yes. I am all for that, but what you plan is totally caper-witted! And if you think I am going to leave you without a word of warning to that scapegrace, my Hope, you aresadly mistaken."

Her eyes shimmering, Hope touched his cheek. "Oh, David, how you prose on. If you wish a word with Nate, I shall certainly not stand in your way, but I will not expose him to his parents. For too long I have run from my problems. I am not running any longer." *Except,* she said added silently, *from you.*

How could she tell him that she had to leave Thorn Hall before she broke down completely? David had been so solicitous of her that her heart fair ached with love, and she had so much love to give. But David was heir to an earldom and would have his choice of brides of proper standing. Why would he want a mere squire's daughter? And there was still Beaucamp to consider.

Grimacing, Hope thought of her mother. Not for her the tactics her mother used to procure her older sisters' their titles. No, seeing the warmth in David's eyes, Hope determined to leave. A small voice inside protested, but she ignored it.

When the snow finally settled and the sun shone warm in the clear afternoon sky, Hope declared it was time for her to return to her responsibilities at Ravenhill. When Lady Thorwall protested, Emily backed her up, declaring in her no-nonsense way, "Time I returned as well."

Carefully, David, his face a grim mask, carried Hope out to the carriage awaiting them. Hope attempted to lighten his mood. "It isn't as bad as all that. After all, I was hired to be a governess to Gwen."

"A job you'd ill need if you would permit me to contact your mother."

"Mother," Hope envisioned her mother's hand in this affair and shuddered. "You won't contact Mother?"

Placing her carefully into the carriage beside the redoubtable Mrs. Barrington, he muttered, "I am a gentleman of my word." Getting in, he sat down opposite them.

Hope could not help but be flattered by the attentions of the viscount, so devastatingly handsome in his tall hat, many caped coat, blue jacket, biscuit-colored pantaloons, and high top boots wet with the melting snow.

Lord, help me do what is right, she cried, but she did not listen for an answer. Instead she turned her head to watch their progress down the winding drive to the newly cleared road. The trees along the way sparkled like diamonds in their coat of ice and snow. Fluffy white stretched unbroken on both sides of the roadway, making Hope sigh. It was so painstakingly beautiful, new, and fresh. She could not help wishing her life was as uncomplicated, as unspoiled. Mayhap she could make the future different from the past, but first, she had to meet her nemesis directly.

At Ravenhill, David carried Hope inside, refusing to set her down until they got to the rose drawing room, whose light summer curtains had been replaced by soft rose velvet ones. The room where the family awaited was warm and inviting, until she spotted Nate.

For a moment, Hope thought she imagined a trace of guilt in his eyes, quickly replaced by mocking amusement as David gently settled her on the divan. "I see our widgeon has returned to the fold, with a gallant no less."

"Hush, Nate," scolded the marchioness, watching the girl's face pale.

Eagerly, Jonathan placed a footstool under Hope's still-bandaged foot. "About time you returned," he said, giving David the cold shoulder.

Gwen rushed to her and would have tripped over her extended foot if David had not grabbed her and swung her up and over. "Careful, Gwen. We mustn't re-injure the ankle."

To the chagrin of the young men, Gwen sat down beside Hope. Giving her a tight hug, she cried, "I am so glad you are back. You are back to stay?"

The marchioness caught Hope glance toward Nathaniel as she answered, "We'll have to see."

Nathaniel inclined his head, and the marchioness glanced toward Carter. He, too, had caught the exchange, and it concerned him more than he wanted Faith to know, not that he could keep anything from her anyway. Something was definitely amiss.

Emily broke the tension. In her direct manner, she stood before the marquess and marchioness. "I want to tender my apologies for behaving in a most encroaching manner. I know I have been trying to control what I had no business controlling and trying to make decisions that were not mine to make."

A faint smile touched her lips as she glanced toward Hope. "Miss Forrest helped me own the truth: I have been running from my grief." Her voice wavered, but she continued bravely, "No, let me finish," she said as the marchioness tried to interrupt. "I ask your forgiveness. If you wish me to leave, I shall. In any case, I will have to return home before the winter properly settles in."

Gracefully getting to her feet, Faith smiled up at the taller woman before giving her a hug. "Of course we forgive you. We do understand, and we do want you to stay as long as possible."

The marquess added, "Apologies accepted." He turned toward Nathaniel. "I don't think you've met my son, Nathaniel, earl of Glynis.

"Nate, Mrs. Barrington, from Boston."

Nate inclined his head. "Ma'am."

"Emily," said the marchioness, "I am glad you returned. I've been thinking you might wish to read the letters father wrote while he was in America."

Emily's face brightened. "I would like that very much."

"Good," responded Faith. "I'll get them out and we can look at them on the morrow, if that would suit you."

For the first time, the women actually seemed to enjoy each other's company and Hope sent up a silent prayer of thanks that things had turned out so well for the American relative. But from the look on Nate's face, it would not be so easy for her.

It did not help that David excused himself, saying he must return home straightway. As he stood up, David glowered at his cousin, puzzling Jonathan and causing Nate to shift uncomfortably. *Surely the chit hadn't said anything, had she?* He would deny everything.

Nate was not, however, prepared for the steel hand on his arm. "Nate, cousin, I will have a word with you before I leave."

"What? Say," Nate grunted as his cousin quietly propelled him from the room.

In the empty library, David thrust his cousin against the wall until Nate felt the imprint of the wainscoting in his back.

"I always knew you for a rotter, Nate, but I did think better of you than the kind of man who accosts innocents in his own household."

"Is that what the over-ripe chit told you?" Nate's sarcasm died in his throat at the rage in his cousin's eyes. "So, that's the way things are. Don't suppose you were man enough to bed her while you had the chance. Ow!" Gingerly Nate touched his jaw. "You didn't have to plant me a facer."

"Then you will apologize. Moreover you will keep your filthy hands to yourself, or so help me, promise or no promise, I shall inform the marquess of your disgusting behavior. . .after I have a bit of a session with you myself." The laconic smile on David's face sent chills down Nate's back. David seldom got angry, but when he did. . . .

"So you promised to keep our little tête-à-tête from my saintly parents. How generous. All right. I apologize. Now get your hands off me."

"And you will keep them to yourself." Releasing Nate, David stepped back.

Straightening his waistcoat and jacket, Nate shrugged. "As you wish. Hardly my type, at any rate."

Leaving the room, Nate started at the swarthy, dark-haired gentleman being led down the hall. "I say, Beaucamp. What brings you here?"

six

"Thought 'twas time for a bit of rustication," Beaucamp laughed smoothly. "Surely this is not your twin."

"Hardly." Nate grinned, "Arland, may I make you known to David, viscount Waverly. David, Sir Arland Beaucamp."

"My lord." Beaucamp's amused perusal of the younger man brought a flush to David's cheeks.

David's eyes darkened at the man's arrogance. "Sir Beaucamp," he managed. "Did the marquess invite you to stay?"

Did he imagine the twitch of a muscle before Nate's growl? "You were leaving, I believe, cousin."

"Ah, yes, but I think I shall take my leave of Hope once more."

"He has a passion for the chit," Nate confided, but Beaucamp scarcely heard. "Hope," he said slowly, "lovely name that. I should like to meet the young lady."

David stiffened at his manner, but Nate only laughed. "Not your type, Beaucamp. Not your type at all. Far too sturdy. Definitely country bred."

"She is all that is lovely." David sputtered, then reddened.

"Of a certain, cousin," Nate scoffed. "Come, Beaucamp. I shall make you known to my family."

David tagged behind as the pair strode toward the parlour. The flunky threw open the door, and Nate swaggered into the room, feeling decidedly bold with the presence of Beaucamp. "Father," he all but crowed, "look who decided to pay us a visit."

David watched the marquess tense. “Sir Beaucamp.” The marquess took the proffered hand. “My dear, Sir Arland Beaucamp, the gentleman who promised to keep Nate from the duns.” David heard the undertone of anger. “Sir Beaucamp, my wife, the marchioness of Aven.”

“Charmed, dear lady.” Beaucamp bowed over her hand.

Quelling the desire to wipe her hand off on the skirt of her burgundy gown, Faith indicated her American relative. “Sir Beaucamp, may I make you acquainted with Mrs. Barrington.”

Again Beaucamp did the pretty, but when Nate went on to introduce his sister Celeste, Beaucamp’s eyes gleamed.

The moment Hope laid eyes on Beaucamp, she gulped a deep, desperate breath. *Oh, Lord, how can he be here?*

Did I not tell you to wait? came the quiet voice.

What am I to do?

Trust me.

“Hope, are you all right?” David sat down beside her. Taking her hand, he found it cold. “Hope.”

“David. Oh, David.”

He responded to her desperate plea, following her gaze to the suave gentleman smoothly trying to charm the ladies.

“What am I to do?” she mouthed, her lies trapping her to silence.

Squeezing her hand, David whispered, “Trust me, Hope. I’ll take care of you.”

Hope’s lips twisted. Trust? She had not done very well on that score. Could she trust David against the likes of the experienced Beaucamp?

At that moment, Nate faced her, a wicked grin on his lips. “Miss Forrest, may I present my friend, Sir Arland Beaucamp. Arland, Miss Hope Forrest.”

Hope did not offer her free hand, but Beaucamp took it anyway and lifted it to his lips. "Miss Forrest, is it?" Danger danced in his eyes. "That's good. Quite good." The promise in his eyes sent a chill down Hope's spine.

"Sir Beaucamp," she murmured, tugging her hand from his grasp.

"So what is this lovely lady doing here?" asked Beaucamp.

Nate sniggered, "That's quite the story, but suffice it to say, Miss Hope is governess to my youngest sister, Gwen—where did she go to? She must have gone up to the nursery."

"Is she younger than your other delightful sister?" The admiring glance Beaucamp sent Celeste's way made the young girl blush furiously.

Hope's stomach turned. Surely Beaucamp wasn't going to turn his attentions toward the innocent Celeste?

With a forced smile, Hope asked, "Sir Beaucamp, I did not know you were a friend of the family. What brings you this way? Rustication hardly seems your style."

Beaucamp smiled languidly at her question. "Had I known Ravenhill hid such lovely treasures, I would have visited Nathaniel before this."

David felt Hope shudder. Nate, too, was less than pleased with his friend's marked attentions toward Hope. Despite David's warning, he had every intention of pursuing the chit. If she truly was enamored of his cousin, she would hardly confess a liaison with him. He licked his lips in anticipation.

He would dearly like to beat out both Jon and David for Hope's affections. Mayhap he would offer marriage after all. It might well please his parents and leave him free to pursue his leisure in London.

Beaucamp's experience might be dashed awkward, and Nate genuinely wished his friend back in London. Then again, if Beaucamp was taken with Celeste, the girl could do worse. Not that Beaucamp would remain faithful—that was not the thing these days anyway—but at least if his friend pursued Celeste, Nate would be free to pursue Hope.

Shaken by the exchange with Beaucamp, Hope wondered how long before he denounced her and explained the truth of the matter to the marquess. Choking back the panic in her throat, Hope asked to be excused. Jonathan and David immediately offered to take her to her room, making Hope blush prettily and Beaucamp raise an eyebrow. So the chit had them all under her thumb. Interesting. Interesting indeed. He'd soon call her bluff.

David lifted Hope in his arms while Jonathan went ahead to clear the way. Once in Hope's room, Jenny quickly sent the young men on there way, but not before David whispered, "I'll be back. Trust me, I'll be back."

Though exhausted, Hope remained too agitated to rest. For two full hours, she tossed and turned in her bed, wondering what to do and praying. Only one answer presented itself. She must avoid Beaucamp as much as possible. With that, her eyes closed and Hope slept.

When Jenny awoke her to dress for dinner, Hope pleaded very real fatigue and had a tray send up instead. Early the next afternoon, Celeste, her face flushed, slipped up to see her.

"I wanted to have a coz this morning," she confessed, "but mother said you were having lessons with Gwen. You didn't have to do that, you know. Mother quite understands you are not up to snuff yet."

"Tsk. Tsk. Such cant phrases. Surely your mother would not approve."

Celeste wrinkled her nose. "It is not so dreadfully wicked or anything. Besides, Sir Beaucamp thought it was rather endearing." She blushed, her eyes dreamy. "He quite discomposes me with his marked attentions. Even Mrs. Barrington has commented upon them." She sighed. "He is so handsome."

Hope's blood ran cold. "Celeste. He is an accomplished flirt. You must not refine too much on his attentions. As a man about town, he is. . .most likely. . .used to having women swoon at his attentions."

Celeste's face darkened. "You're jealous."

"Trust me—" Hope grimaced at the phrase—"I care not a fig for the man, but I know his stamp. I am just asking you to be cautious, use your head, and avoid doing anything that would shame your parents."

"As if I would!" Celeste said, standing up in anger. Then, just as quickly, she settled back down and asked, "Do you really think I am a featherhead, as Jon put it, to throw my cap at the baron?"

Hope groaned at Celeste's cant phrasing, rightly discerning Beaucamp's evil intentions. "You are not a featherhead—just a young woman basking in the attentions of a gentleman who seems all the crack."

"And you say I use cant phrases!"

Hope laughed ruefully, not about to confess how Beaucamp always encouraged her and her sisters' in such petty rebellion. "You will be careful?"

"Please give me some credit, Hope. You act more like my governess than my companion. I am not that much younger than you, yet you sometimes treat me like a child."

Hope bit her lip. Celeste *was* a child by comparison, having no idea how to go on with a rakeshame like Beaucamp. "Just promise you will take care."

"Of course," and with that answer Hope had to be satisfied because the conversation drifted off into more general subjects.

❧

Downstairs, while Jonathan and the marquess were out checking the farms for damage and Nate and Beaucamp were out riding, the marchioness took out her father's carefully preserved letters. They crackled as she slipped them carefully from their envelopes.

"Here is Father's first letter," she explained to Emily. "I was hurt he left me for America when I needed him after Mother's death. It didn't occur to me, however much he loved me, that he could scarce bear the sight of me right then because I reminded him so sharply of her."

She unfolded the parchment with the Boswick insignia.

Dearest Faith,

As you can tell from receiving this letter, I arrived safely in Boston. The trip over was essentially uneventful and I have been made greatly welcome by our American relatives.

Faith read on, selecting the parts she thought would interest Emily.

Will, a slender man of about five and twenty with a long narrow face, is Emily's brother. He has been staying with the Barringtons since taking up his seminary studies. He is almost finished and is temporarily pastoring a small but prestigious Boston church.

Imagine my surprise when I discovered

another of your mother's relatives, another Barrington, when we returned to Boswick Hall after the church service. There in the drawing room in which I first met the family, I met Carl Carlson, a banker originally from Stockholm, Sweden, and his wife, Mignon.

I am sure you recall stories your mother told of her rather wild cousin, Mignon. Well, it turns out she immigrated to America, married Carl, and settled down. . . . Mignon is a Barrington. Her eyes are as startling blue as your own, dear Faith.

Faith's eyes misted and she wiped a hand across her eyes. Clearing her throat, she asked Emily, "What about Carl and Mignon?"

"As you know, despite their advanced age, they had a son, Austin John, while your father was in America. He was Carl's pride and joy. Even Ada reluctantly came to understand their special bond. At least she did once she and Will married. Unfortunately, Carl died while the lad was still in leading strings. Mignon died when he was seven, and Ada and Will took the lad in until he insisted on going out on his own. A responsible young man, he took over the family country place last year."

Well, daughter, this letter has rambled on long enough. In rereading it, I can only wonder what has happened to your usually well-organized father. Catherine says America has a way of changing people.

Take care Faith. . . .

The two women read through the letters, page by page. Tears flowed as shared pain mingled with bittersweet memories.

> *. . . We shall pray war will not come and that cool heads shall prevail. Please do not worry about me staying here. I shall be fine whatever happens. Besides, are we not in the Lord's hands, my dear?*

"Look, Emily. Here's the part about Mignon:"

> *So Mignon is with child, and Catherine is concerned over her because she has little stamina for this ordeal. That is not to say Mignon is not in fairly good health—she is. But still Carlson is torn between excitement and worry. I understand that before he came to America, he lost his first wife in childbirth. Pray that nothing goes wrong.*

Emily wiped a tear. "And nothing did go wrong. Except for Ada."

"Father wrote how she ran off with some bounder who planned on compromising her for her substantial dowry." Faith scanned the pages until she found it. She finished the letter:

> *. . . Despite the threat of war, we are now planning a big wedding and everyone is thrilled, especially Ada. Arlington has left town and there is little doubt he will not be received here again.*

As for Ada, there is a new contentment about her. She knows how foolish she was now by not confiding in us, and she and Mignon have become closer than ever.

One day, Faith, it will be your turn. Whatever happens, never forget that there are those who love you.

Don't ever run from that love or grow bitter.
Affectionately,

"Emily, you have no idea how these letters sustained me," Faith exclaimed. "At the time I was going through a pretty rough time myself." She thought back to the war, to Carter's homecoming, and how she had almost lost him.

. . .So my dear Faith, I am staying. Before he left, William united Catherine and myself in marriage. This may be difficult for you to comprehend, but I love Catherine—though I love your dear departed mother no less. Love is more than holding on, Faith. Sometimes real love also means letting go.

I have released your mother to the Lord. In turn He has given me new happiness, even in the midst of suffering and war.

"Your father was happy with my mother-in-law," Emily said quietly.

"I know," Faith managed through her tears, "but it took me a while to accept that. The war with America was so much more frightening than the war with Napoleon, for it somehow seemed so much closer to me. I guess I resented

Catherine for holding father there when he might have come home. But later I realized how much he needed to be needed."

"And we did need him." Emily bit her lip in a way which reminded Faith of Hope. "Especially after Jeremiah was injured."

When they reached the letter explaining how Jeremiah had been injured, Emily wept openly.

> *It did not take us long to realize that the energetic, boisterous son who had gone off to war with such high hopes was gone forever. The man who now limped among us was a broken man. He had lost several toes on his left foot, two fingers on his left hand,and broken his shoulder, which remained stiff. Actually it was as if his whole body had suffered such damage as to distort the whole.*
>
> *Jeremiah is recovering slowly, but he will never be the same. Emily is the strength of the family now, and Jeremiah seems content to lend his support to whatever decisions she makes. He has regained a certain equilibrium, but the boisterous, headstrong young man I first met is gone, I fear, forever.*
>
> *He is quieter now and, in a way, the relationship between him and Emily seems to have deepened. He spends much time with his children, something he did not do before. I can almost see on his face the promise to them that he will do everything he can to see to it they never suffer as he has done. If so, it is a*

promise he cannot keep, for no life is without its pain and sorrow.

As I have been learning ever since the death of your dear mother, sometimes it is only in times of adversity that we learn who we are and how strong our faith is.

As it says in Romans 8:28, "And we know that all things work together for good to them that love God, to them who are the called according to his purpose."

By this time Faith could scarcely read, and both women clutched damp handkerchiefs. "He did work things out," Emily sniffed.

"When Father died. . . ," Faith began.

"I know." Emily reached out, and the two women clutched each other in tears of healing.

Finally, Faith straightened. "Emily, you don't know how much I appreciated getting that last letter."

"The one we found after the war?"

Nodding, Faith recalled how alone she felt while carrying the twins. How she longed for her father. Faith's hands shook as she unfolded the last letters) one from Emily and one from her father.

. . .Sometime after the death of your father, this was found behind the desk at which he habitually wrote. It was almost as though he left it in the event he did not make it back home. This is but speculation, since we have not opened it. I can only hope it gives you comfort during this time.

Faith began reading her father's last words to her:

> *Dearest Daughter,*
>
> *I have no idea whether or not you will ever read these words, but I thought best to leave word here—just in case.*
>
> *Ever since we have made plans to return to England, I have felt a certain disquiet within. Not that I think this is the wrong thing to do, I do not, but somehow there is a heaviness. Mayhap this comes from leaving a family I have grown to love dearly, but I think it more. . . .*
>
> *I, too, am excited about coming home, but while I try to underplay it, I am well aware of the danger this poses for Jeremiah's friend—and for us.*
>
> *My dear daughter, I know not what God has in store for your future, but I do know it is a future with a love you cannot now even comprehend. Love grows, for the more love we give, always, the more it is returned. That is the key to real love. It is unselfish. Remember always, I love you and Edmund so very, very much.*
>
> *Whatever may happen to me, rest assured I have left you in the best of care, for I have left you in God's hands, and God is always faithful.*
>
> *My love and affection always.*

Folding the letter, Faith slipped it back into its envelope. She choked back the lump in her throat, sensing Emily did the same.

Emily managed to speak first, "Thank you for sharing those with me. It makes all of those dear, departed ones come alive again." With a long finger she traced the pattern on the couch on which they sat. "I had forgotten how hard those times were. How much you, too, have suffered. Ever since Jeremiah died. . . ." She struggled to continue. Not being a demonstrative woman, sharing her heart was especially difficult.

"You have had to be the strong one in the family," Faith acknowledged quietly. "Now the children are grown, and you don't know quite how to go on."

Emily met Faith's compassionate gaze, "Worse. I don't feel wanted any longer. Of course, Robin, at least would claim differently, but he truly does not need me. No matter what, Jeremiah needed me. . .and I needed him. He might have been unable to do much, especially those last years, but he was very wise, and I relied on his advice and counsel." More plaintively than she meant, Emily asked, "What am I to do now?"

Ever since Emily had arrived, Faith had resented her interfering, but now her heart overflowed with love and compassion. Reaching over, she hugged the older woman. "I can't say."

Taking out her father's last letter, she reread slowly, "'I know not what God has in store for your future, but I do know it is a future with a love you cannot now even comprehend. Love grows, for the more love we give, always, the more it is returned. That is the key to real love, it is unselfish.'

"Whatever happens, Emily, remember God loves you and He is in control of your life."

Tears coursing down her cheeks, Emily hugged Faith back. "I know. Thank you, my dear Faith. Thank you." With a sniff, she got to her feet. "Now, if you will excuse me, the

Lord and I have some serious catching up to do."

❧

The next day Hope began hobbling around on her ankle, careful not to re-injure it. David found her in the schoolroom with Gwen. "Hope, what are you doing up?"

At the sound of David's voice, Hope relaxed. The look on her face prompted him to question. "What's wrong?"

"Nothing really," she smiled in welcome. "I fear. . . ." Gwen's eyes upon her caused Hope to amend her sentence. "I thought you might be Nate."

Frowning, David took Hope's arm and insisted she sit down on the wide seat beneath the row of tall windows. "Does he come here often?"

Before she could answer, the door once more swung open, admitting the dark-haired young man. Squealing, Gwen flung herself into his arms. Nate laughingly threw his little sister up into the air, then deftly caught her. He looked so much younger when entertaining his sister. The love in his eyes always softened Hope's feeling toward him.

"I say," said an arrogant voice at the door which made Hope cringe. "Mayhap the child would let me play this game."

Her eyes wide, Gwen clung to her brother. Nate's eyes narrowed. "I think not, Beaucamp." There was no doubt he resented the older man's presence. Then again, Nate resented David's presence, as well. "So cousin, you barged in, too. How cozy we all are."

"And what brings you to the nursery, Lord Beaucamp?" David's stance proclaimed his protection of Hope.

Nonchalantly the baron swept the scene with amused eyes. "'Tis a bit crowded. Mayhap later. I am certain Miss Forrest will attend me. . .eventually."

Hope flushed, while both David and Nate frowned. "I say, Beaucamp." Nate released Gwen, who shrunk away from the look in the newcomer's eyes, "I do not recall extending an invitation to you here."

Seeing Gwen's fright, Hope held out her arms. With her adored brother facing off the stranger, Gwen ran to Hope.

"If you can raid the nursery, Nate, along with your cousin, I supposed I was not intruding," Beaucamp said drily.

Nonplused, Nate gritted his teeth. For all his supposed town bronze, he still felt like the greenest schoolboy when encountering Beaucamp's rejoinders. Abruptly, Nate swung about. "Surely we can find something better to do," he grated, heading for the door. Glancing back, he glared back at his cousin. "David?"

David grinned. "I'll not stay long, Nate."

Hope's deep sigh of relief as the door closed behind Nate and Beaucamp brought a frown to David's face. "I had no idea he was so free with the nursery."

"Nate always comes to see me," said Gwen. "He loves me."

David and Hope exchanged a knowing look. "Yes, Gwen. Nate does come up here," Hope said, adding, "too often."

"You just don't like him to interrupt my lessons." Mischievously, Gwen grinned, "But I do."

A few minutes later as David prepared to take his leave, the door slammed open. "Where is that brother of mine? Is he here again?" Jonathan breathed heavily. "He gave me the slip. David, I had no idea you'd come to visit."

"Nate hadn't expected to find me here either," David said sarcastically. He eyed his cousin thoughtfully. "Come, Jonathan, let's leave Gwen to her lessons. Besides, I have a matter to take up with you concerning that brother of yours."

"David, must you leave?" Both young men heard the tremor in Hope's voice. Jon heard more, and his heart grew heavy with acceptance.

"Hope, I shall see you at luncheon. Aunt Faith asked me

to stay." David basked in the radiance on her face. "Come, Jonathan."

In his bedchamber, Jonathan paced the floor. "I can scarce credit this, that my own brother would accost a young woman in this house."

David's lips tightened. "She almost lost her life trying to get away from his unwanted attentions."

"I had no idea." Jonathan caught his cousin's eye. "She loves you, doesn't she, David?"

"I think so, Jon."

"And you, how do you feel about her?"

"I don't want to hurt you, Jon."

"David, have done. I want the truth of the matter. Are you serious about her? I mean, marriage serious."

His cousin's blunt questioning caught David by surprise and he considered his answer thoughtfully. "Yes. Yes, Jon, I am. Sorry."

Jon's shoulders slumped, then straightened. He shook David's hand. "If she has to have someone other than me, I can't think of a better man I'd want to have her."

A boyish grin spread across David's face. "Thanks, Jon. That means a great deal to me."

Dropping David's hand, Jonathan asked, "So what do we do about Nate? Matters being as they are, I should go to Father."

David frowned. "Mayhap if his lordship were here. . . ."

"Hope needs protection now from that rake of a brother."

"I agree, Jon, but Hope made me promise not to make a case of this. She will not be pleased to know I passed this information on to you." David passed long fingers through his thick, blond hair.

Jonathan raised his arms. "Why ever not! Unless it's all a hum."

"Do you believe that, knowing Hope?"

"No. Never known a chit so honest, other than Celeste and Gwen. Doesn't wish to cause waves, is that it? What balderdash! And you want me to watch out for her."

"Precisely. I cannot be around all the time. As for your father, he cannot do ought until he returns from London."

"I still think we should tell Father when he returns, but for now I shall do as you ask. I certainly would not wish to worry Mother."

❧

Beaucamp's visit to the nursery quite unsettled Hope, and she was hard put to keep her mind on teaching her young charge. Instead, she had Gwen read to her until Celeste returned flushed and excited.

"Hope, Mother says you are to come down for dinner."

Dismayed, Hope said, "I can't walk down all those stairs yet."

"Of a certain, but we'll see you get down to dinner."

Feeling she had been given no choice, Hope settled for a smile, "Dinner it is."

Dressed in a gown of deep rose with bands of lace down the sides of its long sleeves and skirt, slimming her figure and bringing color to her pale cheeks, Hope turned before the mirror.

"Right smart up to mark, Miss Hope," declared Jenny with satisfaction. "I like the way yer hair has been growin' out. And with it brushed just so," Jenny showed her, "your face appears slimmer."

"You're a wonder, Jenny, you truly are." Hope scarce recognized the young woman in the mirror. True, she had lost some weight, but this— She wondered what David would think, then blushed at the thought. As though Hope's thoughts conjured him up, Jenny admitted the young man.

His eyes widened in an appreciation which warmed Hope down to her toes. "Aren't we quite the thing tonight? With your permission, lovely lady." A boyish grin spread across his face.

Hope grinned back. "Milord, at your pleasure."

"My pleasure indeed," said David, deftly picking her up and carrying her from the room.

"I say, Waverly," smirked Beaucamp, "had I known our governess was up to the nines, I'd come for her myself."

At his side, Celeste wilted. "You do look very nice, Hope."

Seeing the girl's hurt, Hope smiled in sympathy. Better Celeste learn now what kind of man was Beaucamp, before she lost her heart completely. Her victory was short-lived, as Beaucamp languidly smiled down at the young girl—lovely in white with a diamond necklace at her throat and a diamond bracelet on her wrist—and added, "But not as lovely as you, my dear."

Celeste glowed under the compliment, which grated against Hope like nails against slate.

David, too, frowned. "Come on."

Nate met them at the stairs. "I meant to come for Hope myself," he grumbled as he followed the others down the stairs.

"I'd never have let him," David whispered in Hope's ear.

Emily and the marchioness greeted Hope as though she had been gone for weeks instead of days. Hope sensed a new bond of understanding between the two older women. At least God had answered that prayer. She chided herself. God answered prayer, but she just didn't listen very well.

She reddened as Jonathan said impatiently, "Hope. Hope are you listening? Bother! You remind me of Gwen. Never listens. Thankfully she's not old enough to dine with us."

"I'm sorry, Jonathan, what did you say?"

He laughed. "Never mind. Doubt I will engender much

attention when David holds you in his arms."

Hope blushed furiously. Was her tendre for David so obvious? She was relieved when David set her down on the settee, then blushed again (or was it still?) when he sat down beside her.

Dinner went relatively well, and afterward the men elected to follow the women to the parlour since David insisted on carrying Hope, though she protested she could walk with support.

There Beaucamp insisted Celeste partner him in a game of whist. Watching, Hope was disturbed at the affection in the girl's eyes and even more so by the predatory gleam on Beaucamp'sface.

Please, she prayed silently, *don't let the situation get out of hand. Please, Lord.*

Later that night she prayed, "Thank You for the lovely evening with David. Oh, Lord, I love him so much and don't know what to do. I want to trust You."

Then why don't you, trust in me with all your heart?

"I am trying, Lord. I am trying. I know You wanted me to stay longer at Thorn Hall, but again I did not listen, and now look at the mess I am in. But I am worried about Celeste. I have to protect her, Lord. You know how Beaucamp is."

And what will you do?

"I don't know."

How about listening to Me?

Hope bit her lip. Hadn't she promised to do just that? "Yes, Lord. I will listen, but please make Your leading clear—I'm not used to listening."

She could almost hear God's chuckle.

But humor was the last thing on Hope's mind several days later when she discovered Celeste struggling in Beaucamp's arms.

seven

"Arland," Hope commanded, "leave her alone."

In confusion, Celeste tried to step from the circle of Beaucamp's arms.

Laconically he smiled, "Jealous, my dear?" His eyes narrowed. "Mayhap you will run to the marchioness."

"Yes, this has gone on long enough."

"And tell her what?" He dared her to answer.

Biting her lips, Hope stared into his lustful eyes and gulped. Panic welled up inside, and all she wanted to do was run. Poised for flight, the inner voice whispered, *And what about Celeste?*

"Celeste, come with me," Hope took her arm. "There is something I need to tell your mother."

"Hope," Beaucamp's smile sent a chill down her back, "are you sure it is not too late?"

"And what do you mean by that!"

"You'll see, soon enough. You'll see." Beaucamp bowed and sauntered from the room.

"What did he mean, Hope?" Celeste questioned.

"More importantly, Celeste, what were you doing?"

The girl stared at her toes. "Hope, I didn't mean. . .I mean, it just sort of happened. One minute we were talking, and the next, he was kissing me."

"You were here alone." Hope released her arm.

"I know." Celeste looked ready to cry. "Oh, Hope. I am so confused. He has been so attentive, I think it rather turned my head. I know I was wrong in meeting him alone, but I thought he was a gentleman."

"And now?"

"I. . .I don't know. I thought a kiss would be. . .be different, but I didn't like it. Then he wouldn't let me go."

"I told you to be careful."

"I know, but I had no idea he would trifle with my affections like that."

"He's a friend of your brother's."

"That should have warned me," Celeste said. "I won't do it again. Not ever."

"Good. But that doesn't excuse either Beaucamp or myself."

"You?" Celeste stared at the Hope's grim face. "What do you have to do with this?"

"More than you know, Celeste. Come. It's time I reveal the truth." Celeste followed the determined Hope from the room.

Asking the marchioness's location from a flunky, Hope proceeded to the blue parlour, where she stopped in shock.

"Hope!"

"Mother!" Dazed, Hope moved forward to receive her mother's stiff, formal embrace, then moved away. "Mother, what brings you here?"

"Why Beaucamp's letter, of course. Now I hear you have lowered yourself to being a governess, of all the noddy-cocked things to do. Running off directly after your betrothal is announced."

"Mother please. I told you—"

"And I am your guardian until you turn twenty-one or marry."

Hope's breath started between her lips. "Mother, I am happy here. Can't you just leave me be?" She knew even before she uttered her plea that her mother had no intention of doing so. The speculative look in her mother's eyes as they took in the well-appointed parlour was all too familiar.

Sickened, Hope dropped onto a nearby chair covered in dainty, blue-flowered silk.

Puzzled, Celeste sat down beside her mother. "I don't understand."

"It seems our guest is a considerable heiress and engaged to Sir Arland Beaucamp."

"Oh, no!" Celeste threw Hope a look of sympathy.

Hope's pale face moved to the marchioness.

Faith noticed the girl's discomfort. Certainly something was amiss. "It also appears that Hope has second thoughts about this arrangement."

"My lady, that's all it ever was," Hope said bitterly, "an arrangement between Beaucamp and Mother. She sought a title and he. . .he only wanted my inheritance to pay off his gambling debts, which are considerable."

Mrs. Forrester appealed to the marchioness. "You see how she is—always the rebellious one. The baron's land marches our own and it was a natural enough arrangement. I am quite within my rights," she added defensively.

"I am sure you are, legally," said the marchioness, wishing Carter were home to deal with the untenable position the encroaching woman had put her in.

The door swung open, and Jonathan and Nate entered with their cousin on their heels. "Mother, David came to see Hope."

Hope's miserable face drew David to her side. "Hope, what's wrong?"

The look on his face gave Mrs. Forrester pause. "Hope, who is this young man?"

Embarrassed, Hope flushed. "Mother, may I make you known to David Fairen, the viscount Waverly."

Taking Mrs. Forrester's hand, David bowed. "My father is the earl of Thorwall. He is brother to Lady Aven." The woman's sudden simpering disgusted him. Turning back toward Hope, he could see how her mother's manner embarrassed her. *Stuff and nonsense,* he thought, *what is she doing here?*

"I say," said Jonathan after all the introductions were completed. "Thought Hope an orphan."

"Hardly," said her mother dryly. "What she neglected to say is that she behaved like the hoyden she is by running away from her betrothed."

"Mother, please," Hope pleaded. "Not here, not now."

David felt helpless to alleviate her distress.

At that moment, Beaucamp strolled into the room. Ignoring the obviously high tension in the room, he greeted Mrs. Forrester with such ardor that she blushed. "Now Arland, leave all that flummery for your intended. I do thank you for alerting me to her direction."

He laughed at the fury he witnessed in Hope's eyes. Insolently he lifted his quizzing glass and looked David up and down. "I look forward to consummating our union," he murmured so only Hope and David could hear.

Nate smirked. "I say. Doing things up a bit brown, isn't it, Hope. Leading cousin David on when Beaucamp has first rights."

Unable to quell her panic, Hope jumped to her feet. "I didn't lead anyone on." Tears rolled down her cheeks. "I won't marry Beaucamp, I won't! He is a horrid man, and I won't marry him."

She faced her mother. "If you push me, I'll run away again." Whirling, Hope ran from the room, then clenched her teeth as the action jarred her still-tender ankle.

Beaucamp grabbed David's arm to keep him from following. "She's mine, Waverly. Let her go." David's shoulders slumped.

Jonathan stared at the delicately carved ceiling while Beaucamp started off on a stream of reminiscences with Hope's mother. No one but David noticed Nate slip from the room and follow Hope.

Nate watched Hope enter her room, then sneak back out with a small valise. Over her afternoon dress she wore a cape. Sunk in her own misery, Hope didn't notice her shadow.

Lord, You failed me. You said You'd take care of me, but You brought mother here. Well, I'd rather die than marry that monster.

Surreptitiously Nate followed Hope down the back stairs and out the door. He caught up with her near the hedgerow.

"Hope."

Horrified, she froze. Nate reached for her, and she slapped him smartly across the face. Picking up her valise, she tried to run, only to trip and fall on the hem of her skirt. Grinning, Nate grabbed for her.

"Leave her be, cousin, or you'll answer to me." David was glad he had obeyed his inner prompting to follow Nate.

Angrily, Nate swung about to face his incensed cousin. "Hope is betrothed to Beaucamp. Her well-being is no concern of yours."

"The well-being of a lady is always the concern of a *gentleman,*" David emphasized as he helped Hope to her feet and held her close.

"How touching," snarled Nate. Pivoting in the powder-like snow, Nate headed back to the house.

"Oh, David, I am so sorry." Desperately, Hope pleaded, "Help me, David. Please help me get away. I promise I'll never bother you again if you help me now."

Groaning, David shook her, his hands hard against her shoulders. "Hope, stop it. Stop it! You can't run. It doesn't solve anything. You must go back."

"No, I won't. I won't marry Beaucamp. I can't."

"Hope, please. Surely there is a better solution than running. Look what it has gotten you so far: the first time you got sick and almost died in the cold rain. The second time you ran, you sprained your ankle. If I hadn't found you when I did. . ."

For a moment, David could not continue. Love for the stubborn girl overwhelmed him. "Hope," he sighed. "You're not going anywhere."

"And if I hadn't run off, I'd be Lady Beaucamp by now." Hope shuddered. "Not that you'd care."

"I do care," David asserted through clenched teeth. "I understand why you ran away from home, but don't run now. You are safer here with the marchioness than any place else. Hope, you have to trust God—and me. Somehow this will work out for the best."

"I've heard that before." Hope brushed her arm across her damp cheeks. "I'll return, since you give me no other choice, but don't ask me to trust you, milord. All I hear you telling me is that I must return to my mother's control and submit to her marriage plans for me."

Shocked by her anger, David protested, "Hope, that's not fair to me."

Throwing back her head, Hope glared at him, her lips thin with determination. "I have nothing more to say. If you please, I shall return to Ravenhill." Unmindful of her sore ankle, Hope stomped back to the house, back to her mother, back to Beaucamp and a future too horrifying to contemplate.

Watching her, David saw her shudder, straighten her shoulders and march up the stairs. Bowing his head, David prayed. "Lord, she is so hurt and confused right now. Please help her to know your love. And Lord," David gulped, "I love her. Help her to understand that I'm doing what is best for her."

David returned to the house, only to take his leave. Beaucamp's mocking mien made his fists ache, but he managed to remain civil. Jonathan walked him to the door, but David was absorbed by his thoughts and said not two words to his cousin.

Emily Barrington, coming downstairs, found the entryway littered with boxes, trunks, and luggage. The servants were all at sixes and sevens. Seeing Jonathan turning from the door, she asked, "What's going on?"

"Hope's mother arrived," he stately flatly. "Seems our little miss is engaged to our latest guest."

"You mean Beaucamp. Well, but what's all this?"

Jonathan shrugged indifferently.

"Miter?" questioned Emily.

"These belong to Mrs. Forrester." The servant's tone left no doubt what he thought of the woman.

"Does the marchioness know about this?"

"Her ladyship is occupied with her many guests," Miter responded evenly.

"I see. I suppose Mrs. Forrester is staying then."

"Too late to send her packing today," Jonathan answered flippantly. "Besides, she is the girl's mother."

Jonathan returned to the parlour, and Miter looked at Emily hopefully. "What am I to do with all this?"

"I guess we had better send Mrs. Haskle to ready a room." With a few deft instructions, Emily had the situation cleared and felt a glow of satisfaction. Maybe she wasn't so useless after all. Perhaps Robin was serious when he said he still needed her to run the household—at least until he married.

For a moment Emily's face darkened, recalling the look on her son's face whenever he looked at the dark-haired Delia. The girl came from a good family, but she was not right for Emily's tender-hearted Robin. Musing that it might be time to return home, Emily went back up the stairs. Passing Hope's door, she stopped. Hope was screaming.

Turning the handle, Emily pushed open the door and hurried into the room. "Hope are you all right?"

Swinging around, Hope faced the older woman. Tears wet her pale cheeks. Her fists clenched. "How could He do this to me. How could He?"

"He who? Sir Beaucamp?"

"Yes—no. Yes, Beaucamp and David and God. Oh, all of them!" Furious, Hope slammed her fist on the arm of the settee, then pulled it back with a grimace. "Ow!"

Emily stilled a smile. "What happened? Does this have to do with your mother arriving?"

"Of course it does. That scoundrel told her where I was."

"I take it you are speaking of your fiancé." Emily sat down in the settee while Hope paced the floor, too angry to stand still.

"He's no fiancé of mine. I don't care what mother says. I'll not marry that monster." She glared toward Emily. "That's what he is, you know, a monster."

"That's why you ran away before we first met. I thought you had stopped running after your last escapade." Emily stared deliberately at Hope's ankle.

"So did I. But that's before God betrayed me. How could He have allowed my mother to come here? I was only safe while I was hidden. You don't know what she is like, always manipulating, always trying to better herself. She managed to secure titles for all three of my sisters, and now she wants to do the same for me."

"So you tried to run again."

"Who told you? David?"

"I guessed. What's this about David?"

"He wouldn't help me."

"Wouldn't help you run away, you mean."

"Same thing."

"Not at all, Hope. David made you come back and face your situation."

"Face it. Face it. No, by coming back, he made sure I will get leg-shackled to that. . .that. . ." Hope ran out of breath as well as words. All her walking had re-injured her ankle, and it throbbed painfully.

"And you think God has let you down by not letting you have your way, is that it?"

Stubbornly, Hope stared out the window. "Mrs. Barrington, I tried to trust God, and look what it got me—Mother and a frightening future with a man I despise."

She shifted her weight to her other foot, but her ankle continued to throb.

"Hope, neither God nor David let you down." Emily patted the seat next to her. "Sit down. I have something to tell you."

Silently Hope hobbled over and sat down, but she stubbornly refused to look at Emily.

"You do remind me of Ada when she was about your age. She so wanted Will to see her as a woman that she wasn't willing to wait for God's timing."

Interested in spite of herself, Hope asked, "What happened?"

"She ran off with some bounder. All she left was a note. That shocked Will, I tell you. Her ladyship's father, my Jeremiah, and Will all rode after her. You see, what Ada didn't know was that this man only wanted her dowry. He figured that if he compromised her, the family would have no choice but to agree to marriage."

"Oh, no!" Hope met Emily's gaze. "Did they. . .did they arrive in time?"

"Just. She learned that she had been very foolish, and it was not a lesson easily forgotten. Ada was always strongheaded." Emily smiled slightly. "Mayhap that is why you so remind me of her."

Hope glanced away, then back. "Did things turn out for her and Will?"

"Yes, they did. She and Will were married."

Hope smiled, "Then everything was all right."

"Not exactly," Emily paused, remembering. She had come to England to forget, not remember. Yet in remembering even the painful times, she was beginning to heal.

"Jeremiah left for the war, now called the War of 1812, before the wedding, and Will followed soon afterward."

"I didn't mean to cause you pain, Mrs. Barrington. Jeremiah was injured, wasn't he?"

"Yes, but worse than his shattered body were his shattered ideals, his shattered faith."

"He didn't have to go to war, did he?"

"No, but he was dead set on going. No one could talk him out of it."

"And Will. Was he stubborn too?"

"He is that," acknowledged Emily, "but his stubbornness is a heart set on following God wherever it leads, even into a fight he didn't truly believe in."

"How did Ada take his going?"

"She was against it, but by then she had learned to trust him and her Lord."

Hope hung her head as Emily continued. "God's ways are not our ways, Hope. He knows that before you can go on with your life, you have to confront your situation, not in your strength and wisdom, but in His. God loves you more than anyone else can, and He has the perfect solution to the problem. But until now, you haven't been willing to wait long enough for Him to work that solution out."

Pausing to determine how her words were being received,

Emily gently placed her hand on Hope's arm. "Remember these verses from the Bible: Romans 8:28 says, 'And we know that all things work together for good to them that love God, to them who are the called according to his purpose.' Then Proverbs 3:5-7 reminds us, 'Trust in the Lord with all thine heart; and lean not unto thine own understanding. In all thy ways acknowledge him,and he shall direct thy paths. Be not wise in thine own eyes: fear the Lord, and depart from evil.'

"Hope, you have been wise in your eyes, trying to work things out in your own way. Has it worked?"

Hope shook her head.

Emily smiled sadly, "I do understand. I was terribly angry with Jeremiah for leaving us as he did, but, when he returned broken in body and spirit, I knew I had to put aside my own resentment to help him." Emily's eyes misted.

"Hope, my dear, my Jeremiah became the kindest, gentlest man you ever saw. Even though I had to be strong and take over many of the things he had done before, I could not have done them without his support or without God's strength. I loved him, Hope. I loved him so much that I was resentful when he died."

She grasped Hope's hand. "My dear, to own the truth, recently I have begun to let God deal with that resentment, let Him heal the hurt I feel."

Hope clasped the older woman's hands. "You have been through so much that my problem seems petty by comparison."

Emily smiled. "No Hope. Each of us has our own path in life, our own pain, our own joys. We must stay focused on the only One who can truly make life worthwhile."

Hope sighed, "It's all about trust, isn't it?"

"I'm afraid so. And Hope, I think you owe God an apology. Would you like to tell Him about it now?"

Nodding, Hope bowed her head. For a moment, nothing came, then through tears of repentance, she placed her life before her heavenly Father, admitting, "Lord, I panic so easily. Help me not to run away again."

The two women hugged before Emily left.

❧

Because of her ankle, Hope was forced to remain upstairs the rest of the day. She was a captive audience for the delighted Gwen. "We will still get to visit Grandfather tomorrow, won't we?" the girl asked.

Hope smiled, "We shall certainly try."

The next morning, Hope felt well enough to see first her mother, then the marchioness. While her mother thought her apology her just due, the marchioness almost made Hope weep all over again with her knowing understanding.

At luncheon when Gwen, who often ate the noon meal with the older family members, announced she and Hope were going to visit the duke, Beaucamp offered to drive them. Hope's face paled so alarmingly, that Nate offered, "What say I drive you, Poppet?"

Gwen clapped her hands, causing her mother to frown at her. Her animation caught Beaucamp's attention, and his eyes narrowed as he studied her. Hatred simmered against Hope for humiliating him in front of the marchioness and Nathaniel. He tried to catch Celeste's eye, but she had been avoiding him. Resentment against the Glynis family simmered. His gaze returned to Gwen speculatively.

Though Hope dreaded driving to the dower house with Nate, Gwen eased the tension with her chatter, causing Nate to respond in kind. As always when he was with his little sister, his eyes lit up and his face lost that bored, man-about-town look. As he lifted Hope down from the carriage, their eyes met in mutual understanding, startling Hope.

Though he appeared pale, the duke welcomed his visitors, and soon they were sitting around a table, laughing and arguing over spillikins. The afternoon passed all too quickly, and they regretfully departed. Nate, glancing up at the darkening skies, urged the horses into a faster clip.

Before they arrived, snowflakes drizzled down on them. Laughing, Gwen caught them in her mouth. Again Hope felt herself softening toward the young man who held his sister in deep affection.

"You are very kind to your sister," Hope said as he dropped her off by the front door.

"Does that mean you will be kind to me?"

Hope flushed angrily. "Why do you have to twist everything I say? You could be a nice person if you'd half try." She flounced off, leaving Nate staring after her, feeling for the first time in years shame at his behavior.

❧

That evening Mrs. Forrester dominated the dinner conversation, making Hope pray she could shrink through the floor. There was no stopping her mother. As soon as possible, Hope escaped to her room and dropped to her knees.

"Lord, help me. I never realized just how odious Mother was until tonight. How the marchioness can put up with her is more than I can understand. Lord, help me be as kind as she is. Help me. Help me learn to love my mother the way I should."

The next few days Hope spent a great deal of time on her knees, for at every turn either her mother or Nate or Beaucamp frustrated her with their manipulations.

Beaucamp tried to center his attentions on Celeste, but when she also spurned him, he turned his anger into a more devious direction.

Jonathan's chill gradually lessened in the face of Hope's growing frustration. "You really don't want to marry that bounder, do you?" he asked when he found himself alone with her in the library one afternoon.

"No, but I have yet to persuade Mother to my case. She is determined that I marry up."

"What about David?"

Biting her lip, Hope turned away so Jonathan would not see the tears sparkling in her eyes. "I fear I treated him dreadfully. I had hoped he would come for a visit so I could apologize."

"I think you're the reason he's staying away. He looked pretty dismal when he left that day."

"Did he tell you what I did?"

Jonathan shook his head. "Why not write him a note of apology and ask him to come over?"

"I'll do that." Hope picked a thin volume from the shelves, then replaced it for another as she browsed.

"I think I know how you can get your mother to cry off the engagement to Beaucamp."

Startled, Hope whirled to look at Jonathan's smug face. "Don't jest. What could possibly—"

"David. He certainly holds you in high esteem. He is heir to an earldom and quite deep in the pockets, which is better than you can say for Beaucamp. Since your mother is such a toadeater. . ." At Hope's grimace, Jonathan recollected with whom he spoke.

"Pardon, Hope, but it certainly is no secret around here. She would certainly go for such an eligible party, and one I am convinced which would find your favor as well." He grinned at her blush.

"Jonathan," Hope told him, "your plan has one major flaw."

"What's that?"

"I will not put David in that position. I will not push marriage on him. Besides, I don't think mother would go back on her word to Beaucamp. I think," she whispered, "she has already given over some of my inheritance. She won't let that go—not mother."

Shaking his head, Jonathan watched Hope march from the room. "I'll never understand women," he muttered.

Not long afterwards, Hope wrote a note for David which she sent over to Thorn Hall with Mrs. Barrington. While Hope had not been to the neighboring property since her accident, all three of the older ladies made an almost daily excursion to Thorn Hall on their way to the nearby village or to the vicarage. Hope began to suspect the marchioness of trying to keep her mother occupied in order to keep her out of trouble. She was much more of a problem than Emily ever had been.

Truth to tell, Emily seemed much more at peace with herself and often talked of booking passage for home. Hope suspected she stayed just so the marchioness would not be left alone to entertain Hope's mother.

Hope thought she should cut everyone's misery short by telling her mother they should return home, but she resisted the temptation, determined this time to wait for God's leading.

The next afternoon, Gwen went with the ladies to Thorn Hall to visit her cousin while Celeste had Jonathan drive her to the village to do some shopping. Both had asked Hope to join them, but Hope declined, not wanting to confess her ankle still bothered her especially in the cold. Out of her window, Hope later observed Beaucamp ride off on a tall chestnut.

Alone, Hope took the opportunity to sit down with the

book she had gotten from the library. She must have read for sometime when she became aware that someone had entered the room. Glancing up, she expected to see Jenny.

"Nate." She got slowly to her feet. Something in his face frightened her. "What are you doing here."

"Everyone prefers my saintly cousin and brother to me. Well, I'm tired of being brushed off by the likes of a lowly governess."

Hope moved backward as Nate approached. She didn't understand the smirk in his eyes until her legs hit the side of the bed. Throwing her book at him, Hope ducked away.

With a growl, Nate tossed the book on the bed and scrambled after Hope. Catching her halfway to the door, he picked her up.Screaming, Hope kicked and beat on his back as he carried her back to the bed and threw her down.

"Let me go! Let me go!"

For a moment they stared at each other. Hope felt panic well up inside. Afraid to close her eyes, she prayed, *Lord, help me. What do I do now?*

Talk to him, came the command. *Talk to him.*

"Nate, why are you hurting me? Do you want to hurt me?"

"I will no longer have Beaucamp or anyone else lording it over me."

Hope struggled to quell her panic as she prayed silently for direction. Then, like a warm refreshing breeze, peace enveloped her. Whatever happened, she knew, absolutely *knew* God was in control.

"Nathaniel, do you really want to be like Beaucamp? Do you really know what he is like, the women he has hurt?"

Horror covered Nate's face.

"You do know, don't you?" she said softly. "Beaucamp is not a man, Nathaniel. He is a beast who preys on helpless women. You are not like him. I see the way you care for your sister. Do you want to hurt her by hurting someone she cares about?"

Nate hesitated, then slowly released her. "I would never hurt Gwen. Not for anything," he said slowly, backing away.

Before Hope could get to her feet, David roared through the open door. "I warned you, Nate."

Nate turned in time to catch a solid left to the jaw.

"David," Hope screamed, "you don't understand."

Rubbing his jaw, Nate headed for the door. "Well, I for one am not sticking around for any explanations." He glared from his cousin to Hope. "You can thank your lucky stars," he growled at Hope as he turned on his heel and left.

"No, Nathaniel, not luck," Hope called after him. "God took care of me."

Puzzled, David asked, "What happened here? When no one was about I came looking for you and found him leaning over the bed. I thought—"

"God happened, David. Nate meant to harm me, but God protected me. He did. He really did!"

Hope came into David's arms like a bird seeking its nest. "I can trust God, and from the way you barged in here," she grinned up at him, "I know I can trust you, too." Her smile faded, "If only you can forgive me."

"Oh, Hope, I forgave you long ago. Don't you know I love you? I want to marry you."

Hope blinked back tears. "And I love you, but Mother—"

Pulling her into his arms, David promised, "Somehow, we'll convince her," and he covered Hope's lips with his own.

eight

Beaucamp, having about enough of rusticating, grew irritated. Somehow he had to get things settled with Hope. From the back of the glistening chestnut, Beaucamp surveyed the well-tended estate, his eyes narrowing in thought. Celeste had a much bigger portion, but she was also younger—too young for a London season.

In his mind he compared the short, sturdy Hope with the tall, dark allure of Celeste. No comparison. Why did he get stuck with Hope? Confound that scheming woman—all because of his minor indiscretion. But for the chit's portion, he would have refused to bow to blackmail. Why had he invited that encroaching woman here of all places?

Beaucamp growled. It was all Hope's fault. He could have had the marriage behind him, had her inheritance in his pocket and his dull wife safely left behind in the north. A slow smile spread on his lips. Mayhap 'twas a good thing he was not yet leg-shackled. By now he could well have run through most of Hope's inheritance, then where would he be? Not only would his pockets be let, but he would have to answer to a shrew of a wife as well. He shuddered at the thought.

Truth to tell, now that he had seen Hope in this new light, he knew they would never suit. How dreadful to have your bride run off when things didn't suit. Why have the rather dumpy Hope when he might contend for the daughter of a marquess?

True, the lovely but haughty—thanks to Hope—Celeste was young, but she was old enough to marry with the permission of the marquess. Especially should they find the girl in a compromising position.

Yes, he would deal with Mrs. Forrester, and then. . . Seeing the curricle returning from the village, Beaucamp urged the chestnut into a ground-eating canter. Pulling up alongside the vehicle, he doffed his top hat. At the sight of him, laughter faded from Celeste's eyes and a frown sat on Jonathan's lips.

"Lady Celeste, Lord Jonathan, I thought I might accompany you back home."

Not seeing any polite way to refuse, Jonathan nodded sharply, "As you wish."

"You are looking lovely as usual, Celeste," Beaucamp murmured her name with a caress that warmed her cheeks.

Observing Beaucamp, Celeste noted his thin lips and the cold expression in his dark eyes and wondered how she could ever have thought him dashingly handsome.

Back at the manor, Beaucamp swung off his horse and hurried to the curricle as soon as Jonathan pulled to a halt. Spanning her waist with his hands, Beaucamp gave Celeste no time to spurn his assistance.

Setting her lightly on the ground, he kept his hands about her tiny waist until Celeste pulled away. Something in his eyes sent alarm bells ringing, and she ignored his proffered arm. "I wouldn't want to put you out," she told him sweetly.

Jonathan could not disguise his grin as his sister took his arm. Behind them, Beaucamp fumed inwardly but started following them up the stairs. Neither by word or gesture would he betray his wrath at the haughty chit.

Before Beaucamp reached the front door, Miter stopped him. "Your mail, m'lord," he said, handing Beaucamp two envelopes. Tucking them into his pocket Beaucamp hurried up to his room and opened his mail. The first letter brought a flush of anger to his face.

"Why can't they wait for their money?" he growled to the empty room. The other letter caused a slow, malicious smile to spread across his face. If his first plan didn't work. . .

At dinner, Beaucamp did the pretty for the older ladies, ignoring Hope and Celeste. Giggling, the two girls slipped away to Celeste's room, done in shades of mauve, blue, and silver.

"What are you going to do about him?" asked Celeste after telling Hope about Beaucamp's gallantry that afternoon.

"I haven't any idea, but I do know one thing," Hope said with new serenity. "God is in control of the situation, and from what He says about marriage in His Word, I know Arland Beaucamp is not the man for me."

"Nor me," declared Celeste. "How he ever took me in with that suave manner, I'll never know."

"You're young, Celeste. And you haven't suffered his petty cruelties the whole of your life."

"Was he really so dreadful?"

Hope told her about her pet. Celeste wiped a tear. "How could your mother—never mind. Anyway, I'd do almost anything to help you."

Hope grinned, "Except marry him yourself."

The younger girl shuddered. "Not that. Thankfully Mother and Father would never allow a match at my age. Actually, I can't see them ever forcing me into a distasteful match, not after what happened to them. They know how important love is to a marriage."

"You have very special parents, Celeste."

"I know, though I don't always show it." Celeste sighed.

"I certainly wish Beaucamp would leave. He makes me feel so uncomfortable. All I want to do is avoid him."

"I know, and I'm afraid avoidance is all we can do at this stage."

Celeste grinned mischievously. "Why don't we take Gwen, and spend the day with grandfather on the morrow?"

Hope grinned back. "Beaucamp won't like that above half."

Giggling, the girls spent the rest of the evening laying out their plans.

❧

The next morning while Celeste and Hope sedately descended the stairs to the carriage, Gwen, her pelisse flowing out behind her, bounced down the stairs after them.

"Nate," she cried, spotting the driver holding in the restless cattle with some difficulty, "are you driving us? I am so glad. Aren't we glad, Celeste, Miss Forrest. . .I mean, Forrester?" Clapping her hands, she raised her arms for her brother to help her into the seat beside him.

Stopping at the bottom stair, Hope quelled the overwhelming desire to run back the way she had come, back to her room. Instead, she gritted her teeth and followed Celeste.

"Nate?"

He caught her eye, then glanced away, but in that glance Hope thought she saw shame. "Miss Forrester," he said formally.

Sensing the tension between Hope and her brother, Celeste remained silent as Nate drove them to the dower house. Gwen, however, chattered the whole way.

Sitting in his combination library and sitting room, the duke welcomed them from his deep russet, wingbacked chair. The duke appeared pale and more tired than usual.

"Your grace," Hope curtsied as Gwen threw her arms

around her grandfather and Celeste pecked him on the cheek.

Celeste also noticed her grandfather's unusual weariness. "Are you feeling all right?" she asked, pulling up a padded footstool to sit near his chair.

"Don't you worry about me, child. Of course, I am fine. Just a might tired today is all." He caught his breath with difficulty.

Hope exchanged a worried look with Nate. She was grateful he took the lead. "We won't stay long, Grandfather."

At Gwen's cry, Celeste told her. "We'll stay a short while, Gwen. Then we must let Grandfather rest."

Patting Gwen on the head, the duke smiled wearily. "There will be another time, dear. Guess I overdid yesterday."

Nate gallantly offered Hope a chair, then pulled one up for himself. "Grandfather, have you seen a doctor?"

"Doctor. Upon my word, Nate, what need I with a physician? Just a bit tired is all. Now don't be flying up in the boughs over such a trifle." The duke rubbed his chest close to his shoulder as though, thought Hope, a sudden pain hit him.

Again she shared a glance with Nate. The young man allowed them to stay but half an hour before having the gig brought around. Gwen pouted as she left but would not openly defy the brother she so adored. This time the silence between Nate, Hope, and Celeste centered on their concern for the duke.

Softly Hope prayed. In the manor entry hall, Celeste took charge of Gwen while Hope spoke to Nate. "He needs a doctor, I think. It could be serious."

"I agree." He averted his eyes from her face. "About yesterday. I. . ." He ground the toe of his boot on the polished inlaid floor. "I am sorry."

"I appreciate that, Nate. But there is someone else to whom you need to apologize."

"David?"

"No, to God. Nate, you are handsome and healthy and have a wonderful family. You are blessed far beyond most, yet you have abused the privileges God has given you. Almost, you became no better than someone of Beaucamp's stamp. How do you wish to be remembered, Nathaniel? As a man who sowed destruction and hurt and cruelty, or as a man who cared, a real man."

Never had he heard these thoughts presented in quite this fashion. Then again, never, admitted Nate, had he been willing to listen. "I'll think on it," he said rather gruffly to disguise the lump in his throat, "but now I need to find Mother and tell her about Grandfather."

"I'll go with you."

Proffering his arm, Nate grinned, "Thanks for the trust."

Hope took his arm. They found the marchioness with Emily in the morning room. When a quick glance about the room failed to reveal the presence of her mother, Hope sighed.

The marchioness's eyebrows rose a fraction at seeing Nate and Hope in such apparent charity with one another. "Nate, Hope. I thought you were all spending the day with Father."

"We thought so, too, Mother, but Grandfather is not well."

The marchioness tensed. "What's wrong? Shall I send for Dr. Meyer?"

"I would advise it, my lady," said Hope. "I fear his grace has a bad heart."

Both Nate and the marchioness stared at her. Emily nodded wisely. "Short of breath, shooting pains in the chest, unusual exhaustion?"

"He has all of those," said Hope, adding, "just like, like a dear friend before he died." She thought of Harry.

The marchioness's face whitened. "Nate, send for Dr.

Meyer straightway."

Halfway to the door, Nate flung back, "I'll go myself. Don't worry mother, it will be all right. It will!"

Setting down the embroidery frame in her hands, the marchioness got to her feet. "If you two will excuse me, I am going to Father. Someone must inform the marquess about his father."

"Don't worry, Faith. I'll take care of things here," Emily told her.

Faith chuckled. "Thanks. I know you keep things under control."

Emily actually turned red, "Only until you return."

"I better go on up to Gwen," said Hope.

In the nursery, Celeste glanced questioningly at Hope.

"Nate's going for the doctor, and your mother's going to see the duke," Hope whispered. "Did you say anything to Gwen?"

Celeste shook her head. Getting up, she whispered back, "I think I'll see if I can go back with mother. She may need me if this is serious."

Nodding, Hope forced a smile to her lips and approached Gwen, who was sitting on the window seat reading a book. Sitting down beside her, Hope said as cheerfully as she could manage, "Time for history, Gwen."

Groaning, Gwen put down her book. For the next couple hours, Hope worked with Gwen, trying not to let her mind wander or her fears overwhelm her. In the weeks she had been with the Fairens, she had come to hold his grace in high esteem and with not a little affection.

When only Hope, Mrs. Forrester, and Mrs. Barrington sat down with her at the table for luncheon, Gwen asked, "Where is everyone? Mother, Celeste, Jon, Nate?"

Emily caught Hope's eyes and shook her head slightly,

but their silent agreement to shield the girl went for naught.

"His grace is in a bad way," Hope's mother told the girl. "Wouldn't be at all surprised to find the marquess the duke soon."

Gwen blanched. "Miss Hope, what is she talking about? I know Grandfather wasn't up to snuff this morning, but. . ."

Hope wished she could allay the girl's fears. Shooting her mother a dark look, Hope said, "It may not be anything serious, but Nate, Celeste, and I thought a doctor should look at your grandfather. That's where the rest of them are now, I suspect."

Tears welled up in Gwen's eyes. "No. No!" Jumping up, she ran from the room.

Observing her with lofty disdain, Mrs. Forrester said, "Hope, can't you even teach her simple manners? But I forget what a hoyden you always were yourself."

"Mother!" Throwing her serviette onto the table, Hope excused herself from the table and hurried after Gwen. She found the little girl curled up in the window seat, staring out toward the dower house whose peak could just be seen over the trees. As Hope groped for the right words, Gwen exclaimed, "Look! They're coming back. They're coming back!"

Tense, Hope stood behind the seated girl, watching the procession return to the manor. When they got close, she took Gwen's hand, and the two girls descended the wide staircase to the foyer.

Hope stepped off the bottom step as Miter opened the door to admit the solemn family members. Gwen flung herself into her mother's arms. "Mother. Is Grandfather all right? Is he?"

The strain of the morning showed on the marchioness's face, and Hope watched with interest as Nate glanced at his mother, then scooped his sister into his arms. "Come, Poppet," he said. "We'll talk about it in the parlour."

When Hope hesitated, Faith smiled, "You too, Hope. After all, you were the one who really understood how serious this was." Her eyes darted around the room. "I suppose we should have Mrs. Barrington with us as well, but. . ."

"I know. You hope to avoid including Mother." Hope was almost beyond embarrassment. "Don't worry. We saw her being driven in the direction of Thorn Hall."

After they were all seated in the parlour, Gwen again made her demand. With a sigh, the marchioness put an arm about her. "Your Grandfather is very ill, Gwen."

"But he is going to get better?"

Faith met the eyes of the others in turn as though searching for some way to soften what she had to say. "I hope so, Gwen, but he has a bad heart. Seems he has known about it for some time but didn't want to worry us." She choked, swallowed, continued. "Gwen, the doctor said your grandfather might go to be with Jesus any time."

"No!" Gwen clenched her fists. "No. I won't let him go. No, it can't be true. Father—Father can make everything all right."

For the first time, Celeste spoke. "We've already sent for Father, but Gwen, there is nothing he can do. Nothing."

Nate squatted down in front of his sister. "Poppet," he told her. "If God calls Grandfather home, we have to let him go, but for now, Grandfather is going to live with us here."

Gwen brightened. "Then he is going to be well again."

"No, Gwen. I don't believe he will ever be well again," Nate told her firmly.

Crying, Gwen beat on her brother's shoulders. Nate only held her more tightly, his face twisted with concern and pain.

"Why?" Gwen cried. "Why is God so cruel?"

"Gwen." The marchioness halted the girl's tirade. "God is not cruel. He loves your grandfather more than anyone can. I know you love Grandfather as well, but you have to let him go. I will not have you act this way before him."

"Look Gwen," Jon told her, "this is a bad pass to be sure." He foundered helplessly.

Collecting herself, the marchioness said, "Gwen, all of us will die at some time or another, and if we love and follow Jesus we will all meet again in heaven."

The muscle on Nate's cheek twitched nervously as his mother continued.

"But Gwen," Faith said, drawing the girl back into her embrace, "God might choose to heal Grandfather. We don't know."

"What can I do?" gulped Gwen.

"What we can all do is pray." The marchioness held her daughter close. "But we must be ready to accept that God's way is best."

Faith sighed at the rebellion in the eyes of her daughter.

"I won't accept it! I won't!" Gwen protested.

Nate frowned in concern, seeing in his sister an unflattering picture of himself. Somehow he had to help her, but how could he when he couldn't even help himself?

Hope's heart softened at the hopelessness on Nate's face.

nine

"No, Sir Beaucamp. I cannot give you leave to approach Celeste on such a matter," the marchioness said sternly, trying not to show the revulsion she felt at the thought. Though she could not put a name to it, something about the top lofty lord disturbed her. For all the baron's high flown airs, Faith still wondered how much he had influenced Nate in his debauchery.

"My daughter is much too young, even for a season, much less an understanding. No, though you might be taken with her at the moment, you shall still have to wait until she has the bronze of a town season behind her. If then she has a partiality toward you, we shall speak again about this matter."

"But. . ."

Gracefully getting to her feet, the marchioness said with finality, "The matter is closed. Besides, I understood you were already spoken for."

Beaucamp's eyes darkened chillingly. "That can be worked out."

"Nonetheless, Sir Beaucamp, until you have settled that matter, you have no right to ask for the hand of another. And now, I must get to the dower house and help his grace move." With that, the marchioness left her guest fuming in the library.

His jaw clenched, Beaucamp stared down into the licking flames of the hearth, his mind churning with hatred and revenge. Point by point he worked out his scheme. If Celeste was not given to him, the top lofty Glynises with their high flown airs would pay, and dearly. The only regret he felt was that they would never know who perpetrated the scheme. Turning, Beaucamp hurried to the door where he snapped impatient fingers at a flunky. "Order my phaeton. I have business in London."

Half an hour later, Nate, hurrying up the stairs, met Beaucamp coming down dressed to the nines in driving jacket, pantaloons, highly polished Hessians, and a many-caped coat. "You leaving, Beaucamp?"

Beaucamp frowned, sensing the young man's relief. "Just going to town on some business. Be back directly—no later than tomorrow morning."

"I see. Until then." Nate proceeded up the stairs, railing against Beaucamp under his breath. The more he saw of his erstwhile friend within the setting of Ravenhill, the less he liked him.

Never again would Nate invite a man of Beaucamp's stamp into the welcoming halls of his home. Strange. He had never felt so protective of his home, his inheritance before. With the duke lying weakly in his bed and the marquess still in London, Nate suddenly realized that he was in charge. He, not Jonathan, would inherit all this.

While before he'd thought only about the monies that would fill his coffers, now Nate understood that being the eldest son held responsibilities as well. Should anything happen to his father, he would be responsible not only for the estate, but for all the people who lived here as well—including his mother and sisters.

With shame, he recalled the debts he had incurred, the money he had taken from Jonathan. Jonathan, who had worked so hard beside his father, would inherit little besides the trust fund. And his sisters, what would they do if he should lose all he gained by inheriting? He thought of Gwen losing her joy for life as a penniless companion or a brow-beaten governess.

In his contemplation, a slight grin twisted his lips. Hope was anything but brow-beaten. Then again, his family was unusually caring, or had been until he came along. All his life he had been jealous of Jonathan, and for what?

Nate sucked in a breath. As though blinders fell from his mind, he finally comprehended how hard his father had tried to reach him and how much his mother loved him. He had repaid them with nothing but grief. What a wasted life!

"Oh, Lord," he groaned, "What have I done?"

He heard his mother's voice telling Gwen, *All of us will die at some time or another, and if we love and follow Jesus, we will all meet again in heaven.*

All but him. Suddenly Nate wanted to make things right. But how? Hope, she would know. He found Hope putting Gwen down for a nap.

"I didn't know she still took naps," he said from the doorway.

"Shh." Hope put her fingers to her lips. "This has all been too much for her. Mrs. Haskle sent up a potion of honey and lemon to soothe her." After tucking the covers over the shoulders of the little girl, whose cheeks showed traces of tears, Hope followed Nate out of the room. Firmly pulling Gwen's door closed, she faced Nathaniel.

"What do you want?" she asked bluntly. Her eyes analyzed Nate's presence.

"Can we sit down?"

Something in his attitude prompted her to do as he bid. As she settled onto the window seat, Nate pulled up the ancient, but sturdy rocker. "Hope, I know you have no reason to trust me, but I have something to ask you. Mother is busy and Celeste has gone to her room. Jonathan went to meet Father." He searched for words.

"I, ah, know I haven't been the best person in the world. I mean, well. . ." He raked trembling fingers through his dark hair. "You started me looking at myself, my life—such as it is. I have been so jealous of Jonathan all these years. I never saw how much Mother and Father really cared about me. And Grandfather—he always treated me well, but I only tolerated him for Gwen's sake.

"Now with him like he is. Hope, if something happened to Father, I would be responsible for all this." He stretched out his arms. "It's frightening. I never really considered the consequences of my inheritance before."

"And now?" asked Hope.

"Now," Nate said slowly, "I am wondering if some of my rebellion was against having to be responsible. The first time I recall anyone saying anything about it, I was still in leading strings. Mayhap all of five. I think I was with Grandmother. She said I must be a good boy and learn all I could because I had to take charge one day."

"And it frightened you?" Hope leaned forward, beginning to understand.

Nate nodded. "Grandfather and Father were so big, so in charge, so strong to a small boy. How could I ever be like them?"

"So you did everything you could not to be like them."

"Precisely. Only now. . ." He sighed. "I've wasted my life. I let men like Beaucamp guide my life. Not that it's their fault—I made the choice. Earlier when Mother told Gwen about meeting in heaven," he laughed softly at himself, "I knew I wasn't part of the family that would meet again."

"You can be," Hope said softly. "No matter what you have

done, Jesus loves you. Nate, you've been running away in your own way just like I ran away from home to escape Beaucamp. That's right," she added at his startled exclamation. "I ran way because of him, but running away doesn't solve anything. I certainly found that out," she admitted dryly.

Nate nodded thoughtfully, then declared, "I am not shirking my responsibilities any longer. Ravenhill is my past, my inheritance, and the future of our family, and I will see that no one, including myself, destroys that heritage." He seemed to grow in maturity even as he made his commitment.

"What about your spiritual heritage? Are you going to embrace that as well? All it takes is acknowledging your sin and accepting the gift of life from the one who died and rose again for you."

"To own the truth, I've done my best to become what Father's—and my—," the thought brought a shame-faced smile to his face, "tenants believed of me. That I was nothing but a scapegrace, a scoundrel."

"You can change all that right now, Nate."

"I certainly intend to do so. I shall be so diligent in my responsibilities, everyone will be seriously put aflutter." Some of his arrogance was returning.

"You can't do it on your own, Nate. You need Jesus' help to change, change where it really counts—on the inside."

"I shall think on it, Hope." He raised his head. A smile tickled his lips. "Who would have thought I would ever have this conversation with you? Almost you persuaded me to believe, but I have a whole lifetime ahead of me to make a decision."

Make it clear, Hope. He needs the truth.

"Nate, God does not promise tomorrow. Today is the day of salvation. Today."

Nate shook his head, "Not now, Hope. I have too much living to do." His fingers brushed her cheek.

Hope turned away. "Oh, Nate."

He sobered, "Don't worry, Hope. Never again. . . ."

She understood.

Leaving shortly thereafter, Nate held the door for Mrs. Forrester who bustled into the room, her face wreathed in a smile that brought a frown to Hope's face. "Mother, what is it?"

"Daughter, it is beyond wonderful. Such a naughty girl you were to run away, but you're a sly one, you are."

"Shh. Gwen's asleep." Hope tried to hush her mother's strident voice.

Quieting, Mrs. Forrester took the rocker vacated by the earl. "Daughter, I can't believe it. That nice young man actually asked for your hand."

"Lord Waverly?"

"La, of a certain." She looked her daughter up and down "Who would have thought it, but of course I have to admit," her nervous fingers tucked a stray curl behind her daughter's ear, "that dress does wonders for your figure And your hair, Umm. I like the style."

"Mother, please. What about David?"

"He asked for your hand, and I agreed. After some persuasion, you understand. After all, I had to refill the family's pockets."

"If you hadn't loaned money to Arland—"

"But the engagement was all set, and I saw no reason not to keep him out of fleet."

"If you had only listened."

"I know, I know, but how was I to know you would find yourself such a prime candidate as the viscount? Someday you'll be a countess. Why you did as well for yourself as I did for your sisters. Course, your father always did say you had a head on your shoulders."

Hope interrupted. "What about Beaucamp?"

Her mother waved an airy hand. "Not to worry. Your young man promised to pay him off."

"You didn't agree to that!" Hope said, aghast.

"Why ever not? The viscount is coop-a-hoop over you."

"It's not right."

Getting up, Mrs. Forrester patted her daughter on the head. "Now daughter, you leave these things to me." With that she flounced from the room.

Shaking her head, Hope went to her room to dress for dinner. Jenny had just put the final touch on her hair, when Celeste scratched at the door, then opened it.

Seeing the girl's white face, Hope asked, "Celeste, what's wrong?" Neither girl saw Gwen, still rubbing her eyes, sidle into the room behind her.

"Grandfather, he's too weak to move." Celeste gulped. "Mother and Father are staying with him tonight. They say," she gulped again. "The doctor told them it is just a matter of time. Jon rode to tell Uncle Edmund and Aunt Celeste."

"No!"

The girls whirled at Gwen's scream. It took both of them to calm her down. Both stayed with the inconsolable Gwen instead of having dinner downstairs.

Celeste stayed long after they had put Gwen to bed, and it was late when Hope finally got to bed and almost dawn before she dropped into a restless sleep.

David wanted her! He had even persuaded her mother to his side, but the fact remained, her mother had given her word to Beaucamp. And, if Hope was any judge of character at all, the man was not about to give up her inheritance, especially since Celeste could not be drawn into his clutches.

"Thank You for Celeste's safety, Lord," she breathed. "Please work things out for David and me, despite Mother."

The next morning, Beaucamp returned from London, catching Hope, Celeste, and Emily at breakfast. "Good morning, ladies," he said, bestowing a smile that did not reach his eyes. Filling a plate, he sat next to Celeste at the table, much to her dismay.

Scarcely had he sat down when Nate rushed into the room, his arm around his ashen-faced younger sister. "Come, Celeste, Emily, you too, Hope. Grandfather is dying, and we must go to him straightway."

Her face pale, Celeste gracefully got to her feet. "Jon?"

"He's with Grandfather now."

A curricle awaited them as they rushed down the front stairs. Tossing Gwen lightly onto the seat, Nate turned to assist the girls before swinging into the driver's perch and taking the reins himself. Snapping the whip over the heads of the lively blood cattle, the earl urged them into a ground-eating canter. Hope sent up a prayer of thankfulness that the day was clear, if cold.

Reaching the dower house, Nathaniel helped the ladies from the vehicle, then swung Gwen to the ground. Taking her hand, he led the way up the stairs and into the silent hall.

Jonathan waited for them outside the door, his eyes suspiciously damp. "Is he. . .?" asked Celeste.

"Still hanging on," Jon told her. "Go on in."

Silently they filed into the room. Hope hung back with Emily, giving the family privacy with the dying man. Lying in the huge, four-poster bed hung with royal blue curtains with gold edging, the duke of Glynmouth smiled weakly at those gathered around him. Quietly he spoke with each, and while Gwen's hands clenched at her side, she made no sound, no sound at all. The others held back tears as they said good-bye.

The duke's voice grew stronger as he spoke with Nathaniel. "Son, I want to meet you in the morning. Don't fail me. Jesus is the only way."

Stepping back, the marchioness motioned for Emily, then Hope. Taking the duke's thin hand in hers, Hope silently shared her deep affection. Struggling now for breath, the duke whispered, "Help her, Hope, help Gwen. It is going to be hard on her. Take care of her."

"I'll do my best, your grace," Hope managed, choking back tears.

"Good," he nodded. "Carter."

Hope retreated, leaving the duke with his son. Faith stood between her daughters, her hand gripping Celeste's, but Gwen spurned her mother's comforting arm. Faith's eyes pleaded with Hope. Gwen was holding tightly to Nate's arm as Hope crossed over to the little girl. Hope and Nate exchanged looks of concern for Gwen over her head.

A long sigh issued from the bed, and Hope knew, even before Carter turned, that the third duke of Glynmouth was gone. Tears coursed unashamed down Carter's cheeks. Her arms out, Faith reached to hold him close. Emily enfolded Celeste, whose sobs filled the room. Jon stiffened. Nate's face hardened.

Suddenly Gwen screamed. "No! No!" Before either Hope or Nate could react, Gwen bolted from the room.

ten

Hope followed Nate out the room in pursuit of Gwen as Emily turned to Celeste and Jonathan. "Why don't we leave your parents and return to Ravenhill? There is much that needs to be done." She caught Faith's eye, "With your permission."

Thankfulness shown in Faith's eyes. "Please," she choked out. "You will let my brother. . .know."

Emily escorted the two young people out of the room and down to the front door where they joined Nate, Hope, and a tight-lipped Gwen.

Nate kept Gwen next to him as he drove the somber group back to the manor. Inside the entry hall, he gave orders for someone to inform the earl and countess and motioned Hope to follow him to the nursery.

Mrs. Forrest stopped them halfway up the stairs. "What's going on? What's happened? Where is everyone?"

"His grace is dead," Hope told her flatly.

Her mother looked over Nate approvingly, "And you are the new marquess."

Grinding his teeth, Nate all but pushed passed her. "Come on, Hope."

Mortified at her mother's behavior, Hope accompanied Nate. She heard Celeste close the door to her room. Emily, she knew, was in her element, organizing the household for the coming funeral.

Once in the nursery, Gwen stared at Nate with hard eyes. Then harsh words began pouring out. "Why couldn't you help Grandfather? Why? If you loved Jesus, he wouldn't have died."

Squatting down, Nate tried to reason with her, but Gwen would have none of it. Casting Hope a desperate plea, Nate got up. "Gwen."

"Go away," she cried. "You killed grandfather. You worried him with the things you did in London. You would not love Jesus."

Nate paled. There was enough truth to his sister's words to cause him deep pain. Shoulders slumped, he advanced toward the door.

Grabbing the girl's shoulder, Hope ordered. "You will say you are sorry, Gwen. Now."

Sullenly, Gwen mumbled, "Sorry." She paused and added, "Go away." Her fisted hand wiped an angry tear. Nate glanced at Hope, who nodded.

"I'll go, Gwen, but I do love you. If you need me, I'll come back."

The click of the door broke the little girl's reserve. Floodgates opened, and tears ran down her white cheeks and splashed on the front of her jonquil gown with its rows of intricate lace and buttons.

Picking up the weeping girl, Hope sat down with her in the oak rocker, holding the girl until she cried herself to sleep. Even as Hope carefully tucked Gwen into her bed, the little girl whimpered, and Hope, not wanting to leave her, returned to the sitting room and sat down in the window seat.

A floor below her, Celeste opened the door to the scratch."Beaucamp." Wiping her eyes, she tried to smile, "I am sorry, but I am not up to seeing you now."

The expression on his face frightened her, and she stepped back as he pushed into the room, closing the door firmly behind him. His eyes narrowed. "I am giving you one last chance, my dear. Will you marry me?"

"Get out!" she cried. "I wouldn't marry you if you were the last man on earth."

The flash in his eyes told her she had gone too far. Silently, she cried out, *Lord, Jesus, help me!*

"Celeste. Celeste, dear," came Emily's voice outside the bedroom door. "I was wondering if I could ask you a few questions about the arrangements that need to be made."

"Yes, Aunt Emily. Yes, I'll be glad to help," Celeste answered, breathing a prayer of thanks.

"You'll regret this," Beaucamp hissed. He opened the door to the hallway and hastily retreated, angry that his attempts to gain Celeste had failed. It was time for vengeance against this all-too-proud family. He headed toward the nursery.

Meanwhile, Celeste retreated from the sitting room to her bedroom and opened its door to the hall, attempting to appear as if all was normal as she answered her aunt's questions. Celeste recognized that the older woman had enough on her mind without being burdened with someone else's problems. Instead, she waited until her aunt took her leave, and then headed toward Jon's room. Turning a corner, Celeste stood face to face with Nate.

"Celeste, I am truly sorry about Grandfather, you know. I know how much you cared about him."

Nate's unusual solicitude broke her control, and Celeste flung herself against her astonished brother. "Nate. Nate! How could you have brought him here?"

Accused for the second time, Nathaniel grimaced. "What's this?" He pushed his weeping sister away to look into her face. "Who are you talking about?"

"Beaucamp. He came to my room and he. . .he was not a gentleman." She gulped. Nate handed her the kerchief from his pocket. "Nate, he threatened to get even."

"What?" roared Nate. Escorting her into his room, Nate

demanded the whole of the matter, his face growing colder with each revelation.

"He's gone!" Nate declared. "I'll see he never shows his face here again."

"Nate," Celeste's soft voice stopped him at the door. "Thank you."

Her gratitude warmed him as no amount of liquor had ever done. "Stay here, Celeste. I'll be back shortly."

❧

Upstairs, Hope admitted Jonathan to the nursery.

"Your mother wishes to see you, Hope."

"Gwen cried herself to sleep, and I don't want to leave her."

"I'll stay." Jonathan plunked himself down on the window seat.

Down the hallway from her mother's room, Hope met Beaucamp charging toward her. "Hope."

He grabbed her arm. "So you think you can escape me, do you? If you think I'll let that hair-brained mother of yours nullify our agreement, you have bats in the cockloft."

"Let me go. Lord Waverly is more man than you'll ever be, Beaucamp, and you'll never even know why."

"But you belong to me."

"Never."

"I would not be so sure if I were you. Your mother has an arrangement with me she will find difficult to break." From his pocket, Beaucamp pulled out a piece of paper and let it unfold before her eyes.

"A marriage contract," she whispered.

"Signed and witnessed." He stuck it back into his pocket. "However much your mother wishes to renege, she cannot break this agreement."

Hope's heart sunk. "She never told me."

"You ran away, remember?"

"And you didn't want to reveal it as long as you thought you might have your way with Celeste."

The twitch of his left cheek revealed the truth of the matter. "We shall marry as soon as possible, Hope. Now I want you to inform your mother that we are leaving for the north country at first light."

"I won't!" Hope felt the panic rising, the overwhelming desire to run. *You will help Gwen,* she remembered the old duke asking. And she had promised.

Trust Me, A sense of peace calmed her.

"We must wait at least until the funeral. I promised his grace to stay with Gwen."

"We shall see," Beaucamp pushed past her. "We shall see."

Hope's mother lay on the couch with a cloth over her eyes. "Dear me. I can't take all this excitement. Daughter, about your intended," she murmured, opening her eyes.

"Which one, Mother?" Hope asked with a note of sarcasm.

"Beaucamp. I fear I was rather premature in giving my blessing to Lord Waverly. Beaucamp assured me he had other plans, but now he says he'll not give you up."

"Mother, how could you have signed a contract without even telling me? You two had it all worked out. If he got Celeste, I got David, but it doesn't fly. Celeste won't have him. No decent woman would."

Her mother stiffened. "I did what I thought best."

Hope rolled her eyes. "I will not marry Beaucamp."

"Hope," her mother sighed, "you have no choice."

"There has got to be some way."

"No, it's legal."

Holding in her scream of denial, Hope rushed from the room and up the stairs where she collided with Nate.

"Hope. I thought you were with Gwen," he said with dismay. "You didn't leave Gwen alone?"

"Of course not, I left Jon with her."

Gulping, Nate closed his eyes, "If anything happened to her. . ."

"What is it, Nate. What's wrong?"

For answer he handed her a letter. "I went to Beaucamp's room to confront him. He wasn't there, but I found this letter. I won't have you read it—it's no reading fit for a lady—but it reveals that Beaucamp has been supplying innocent girls as young as ten for. . .for a notorious house in London."

Hope blanched. "Gwen?"

Together they ran up the stairs. Flinging open the door, they found Celeste bending over her prostrate brother. "I came to talk with you, Hope, and I found Jon like this."

Nate ran over and jerked open Gwen's door. "Where is she?" he demanded.

"I left her asleep," said Hope.

"I haven't seen her," said Celeste, not yet comprehending.

Groaning, Jon held a blood-soaked cloth to his head. Seeing the concerned faces around him, he sat up. "Gwen," he ground out. "Beaucamp took Gwen."

Without another word, Nate pivoted and ran from the room.

Hope stared after him. "We have to get help," she told the other two. "Beaucamp is kidnapping Gwen."

"But why?" Jonathan asked.

Celeste knew. "Revenge. He won't get far. Father will pay."

"You don't understand," Hope almost whispered. "He plans on losing her in a notorious house in London."

Jon got to his feet, swaying dizzily. Celeste sat him down again. "I knew he was no good. I have to go after them."

"You are in no condition to go Jon." Hope told him. "Celeste, get Jenny to take care of him. Do you think you could get help from your uncle?"

"Of course. And you?"

"I promised the duke to watch out for Gwen, and I will. . .with God's help," Hope amended. Glancing out the window, she cried. "There they are!"

Celeste came to stand beside her. "And look. Way up there, near the road. It's a closed carriage."

"Gwen is fighting him," Hope told Jon. "It's causing the horse to stumble."

Jonathan shook his head, then groaned. "Both of you go find Uncle Edmund and David. You can't do this on your own."

Hope ached to defy him, but stopped. "Come Celeste."

Rushing as fast as possible, the two girls ran for the stables. Halfway there, David met them. Swinging down from his gig, he drew both girls into his arms. "I'm sorry about your grandfather, Celeste. I came over as soon as the news came. My parents will follow."

"David, thank God you are here." Celeste was almost incoherent.

Hope explained, "Beaucamp has Gwen."

A moment later both girls found themselves beside David in the gig. "We'll find him."

Turning the grays about, David headed them in the direction Hope pointed. "David," she swallowed with difficulty. "There's something else."

"What?" He didn't take the time to look at her drawn face.

"I can't marry you. Mother didn't tell you—or me—that she had already signed a marriage contract with Beaucamp. He showed it to me just a while ago. It's in his pocket. It's legal. 'Tis binding. And I will be forced to marry him."

"No!" grated David. "I will find a way to stop him."

There was no more time for discussion. Up ahead they could see Beaucamp riding neck or nothing with Nate in hot pursuit.

eleven

Rage coursed through Nathaniel as he urged his large black after the smaller mare chosen by Beaucamp. The breeze flung back Gwen's anguished cry, "Nate. Nate, help me!"

Leaning forward, Nate spoke to the black and felt the prime blood cattle respond. Far ahead, he glimpsed the shabby closed carriage. Seeing Beaucamp, a burly man swung down from beside the coachmen and opened the door.

Screaming, Gwen clamped her teeth down on Beaucamp's hand. He slapped her so hard that Gwen's head snapped back. His hands full of the squirming girl, Beaucamp could not ply his whip.

"Nate's catching up," Gwen yelled into her captor's face, "and when he does, you'll pay for what you've done." Then she recalled how she had sent Nate off and choked back a sob.

"Stop, Beaucamp," Nate yelled from two horse lengths back. "You can't get away with this."

For answer, Beaucamp clamped one arm around Gwen. Reaching into the deep pocket of his jacket, he drew out an ornate pistol and aimed it at Nate, whose black galloped alongside, stride for stride.

Laying the ribbons over the black's neck, Nate grabbed for the pistol. Seeing his plan go askew, Beaucamp fought viciously, trying to dislodge the marquess from his horse. Unsuccessful, Beaucamp used the pistol to swipe at the black's head, causing the horse to shy and rear. For precious moments, Nate fell behind while regaining control of his horse.

Then he honed in on Beaucamp, catching him as he again clutched the struggling Gwen.

"Nate. Be careful!" she screamed.

This time, Nate succeeded in grabbing the gun out of the man's hands. He managed to drop it into his pocket before seizing the reins. Jerking the mare to a halt, Nate tackled Beaucamp. Tossing aside the girl, who landed with a thump, Beaucamp swung on Nate, only to meet the marquess's fist.

Fury flared in Beaucamp's eyes. Ducking, he grabbed for Nate's throat. For a moment, his hands clutched the marquess's neck.

"No!" Dizzy from her fall, Gwen tried to get to her feet, then fell in a heap as tears streaked her face.

"I'll have the girl yet," Beaucamp growled.

"No!" gurgled Nate. Lunging forward, his unexpected action dislodged Beaucamp, whose hands dropped from Nate's throat. Neighing in fright, the smaller mare tried to rear. Unbalanced, Beaucamp grabbed for the horse's flying mane. Propelled by his hatred for Beaucamp and concern for Gwen, Nate hurled himself at Beaucamp, knocking them both to the ground.

Gwen started for the men. "Nate, are you all right?"

"Watch out, Gwen!" he yelled and then prayed, "Lord, help her. Protect her."

The warning came too late. Grabbing the terrified child, Beaucamp dragged her kicking and screaming the few yards left to the carriage. "Blast it, man!" he growled at the driver. "Throw me a gun."

David and the girls watched as the gun curved through the air and landed in Beaucamp's outstretched hand. As if in slow motion, they saw Beaucamp's neat turn, his careful aim of the gun, and the shot fired off.

"Nate!" Gwen screamed.

Her brother fell back.

"Nate!" Celeste echoed.

"Beaucamp," ordered David as the horses roared forward, "Leave her be."

At the sight of the gig, the hired lackey slammed shut the carriage door, swung up beside the driver, and yelled, "Come on. Let's get out of here while we can."

They ignored Beaucamp's roar of rage. Then, as though realizing his own danger, Beaucamp flung Gwen from him and tried to run. Too late.

Handing the reins to Celeste, whom he knew to be a respectable whip, David leaped from the vehicle, knocking Beaucamp to the ground. The gun flew from Beaucamp's hand. Quickly, Celeste pulled up the horses to go to the assistance of her brother, who was slowly dragging himself forward.

Seeing his last chance fade, Beaucamp twisted away from David. Grabbing the dazed Gwen, he put a strangle hold on her. "Let me go," he heaved, trying to catch his breath.

Cautiously David moved forward. "Give it up, Beaucamp."

"If you come any closer, I'll snap her neck," he growled. Seeing Hope, a malicious smile touched his lips. "Hope, I'll let her go if you agree to come with me. . .now."

"Never," said David.

"I haven't much to lose," Beaucamp grunted, bending Gwen's neck farther.

Hope's heart pounded. If ever she wanted to run, this was the time. She knew Beaucamp. His was not an idle jest. *Lord, this time I trust,* she prayed.

With a calmness that earned admiration from those watching, Hope climbed from the gig and walked toward Beaucamp. Her dreams lay in ashes. David tried to stop her, but Beaucamp held them to their places with his threat.

"No, Hope, you can't. What about us?" David whispered through dry lips.

"God is in control, David, and, this time I am not running away."

Beaucamp licked his lips. "Good Hope. Now you must make the others promise to stay put and not follow. After all," he grinned, "I have the paper to prove you belong to me."

"I'll go with you, Beaucamp, but you must let Gwen go." At any other time the look in the man's eyes would have sent Hope screaming, but now she stood her ground.

All eyes were so intent on the drama playing out before them that no one noticed Nate reach into his pocket.

Two steps from Beaucamp, Hope waited. "Now, Beaucamp. Or I walk away."

Doubt flickered across Beaucamp's face at this new, confident Hope. He flung Gwen down and reached for his intended. In that moment, Nate aimed and fired. Dropping Hope's arm,Beaucamp spun around, surprise and shock on his face as his hand went to his shoulder.

David rushed in. Grabbing Beaucamp, he jerked open his jacket and found the contract. Pulling it out, he tore it into little pieces and threw it up for the wind to carry away.

"There Beaucamp. Hope is free of you forever. Though I'd like to see you hang, I'll give you one chance and one chance only to walk away so there will be no scandal."

For a moment Beaucamp hesitated; then with a growl of defeat, he turned and limped away.

As David gathered Hope into his arms, Gwen cried, "Nate! Oh, help!"

Swinging about, David and Hope rushed to where Gwen and Celeste knelt beside the fallen man.

twelve

Nate lay on the ground, blood covering the front of his shirt and waistcoat until it was impossible to know where he had been injured. Moaning, Gwen held his head in her lap, begging the others to help him. Grabbing up her skirt, Celeste ripped her petticoat into strips which she used to try and staunch the blood.

"We have to get him home," said Hope.

David glanced from his gig to his tall, nearly unconscious cousin. "It's not going to be easy. I'll need all the help I can get, but there is no room for all of us."

The sound of hoofbeats startled them to attention. Celeste shaded her eyes against the bright sunlight. "It's Jonathan."

Sporting a raffish bandage around his head, Jonathan pulled up his horse and slid to the ground. "Nate." He kneeled beside his brother. "What happened here?"

Tersely David explained. "We must get him home."

Jonathan eyed the gig. "Look, David. You handle those ribbons, and I'll hold Nate. Celeste, you take the horse and go for Dr. Meyer."

"We can't leave Hope and Gwen," protested David.

Hope drew Gwen to her feet. "This is no time to quibble. Jon, take your brother. Go, all of you. Gwen and I will head back on our own. Once you get Nate taken care of, send someone back for us."

Giving her a quick hug, David helped Jon lift Nate onto the gig, then swung up to take the reins. Celeste was already far down the path on the galloping bay. "I'll return as soon as possible," David told her.

Watching them drive away, Gwen clung to Hope. "Why was I so cruel to Nate? Why? Is he going to die? Is God punishing me for what I said?"

Holding the girl, Hope started walking back to Ravenhill. Rustling in the underbrush caused her to glance around nervously and hurry her stride. What if Beaucamp caught them out here alone? Biting her lip, she prayed silently not only for their safety, but also for wisdom to answer the hurting child.

"Gwen, there are times all of us say or do things because we're hurt or we're afraid. This morning when you lashed out at your brother, you were running away from the pain of your grandfather's death. You hurt Nate, yes, but I am certain he also understood.

"Gwen, dear, I don't know what will happen to Nathaniel, but I do know God loves him very much. God loves you, too, Gwen, and I do not believe this all happened to punish you. What happened came from some very wrong choices made mostly by Beaucamp, but also by your brother."

"But. . .but what if he dies, Miss Forrester? He doesn't know Jesus." Anguish twisted the features on Gwen's ashen face.

"Then we must pray for him, Gwen. And leave the rest in God's hands."

Hope led the little girl in prayer, praying for each family member in turn and especially for Nate and his need of a Savior. Gwen was flagging, exhausted from her ordeal, when David pulled up with the gig and helped them aboard.

"How's Nate?" Hope asked.

David glanced from Hope to Gwen and shook his head. "Not good." They finished the trip in silence.

Back at Ravenhill, Hope took Gwen to the nursery, but the little girl would only go when Hope promised not to leave her and David promised to inform them of any change in Nate's condition.

Upstairs, Gwen climbed in Hope's lap and let Hope hold and rock her as though she were a toddler. But her body was tense and her face streaked with tears, and it was difficult to hold her comfortably. Hope prayed as they waited.

Jenny offered to get a tray, but neither girl could eat. Still they waited. Gwen's eyes closed, then popped open as if by sheer force she kept herself from falling asleep.

"The duke and duchess are with him now," Jenny told them. "After the death of the old duke, I fear this is almost more than her grace can bear. Nate was always her favorite."

"Was," wailed Gwen.

"He's still with us," the maid hastened to assure them, "but I fear 'tis bad. The earl and countess are here as well. They all want to know what happened."

Hope pressed her lips together, unwilling to enlighten her. David had told her that he and Jonathan had decided Jon's parents need not know the full truth of the matter. They let the assumption stand that the shooting was simply an unfortunate accident.

Hope prayed they were doing the right thing by not owning the truth. By her sense of justice, Beaucamp should be caught and hung for his crimes, but she also understood the pain the household was already suffering. They did not need a scandal which might reflect negatively on both their daughters.

"Lord, help us," She petitioned over and over.

The sun had dipped behind the horizon when David made his way to the nursery. His face was pale, and a hint of moisture shown in his eyes.

"Nate?" Gwen cried.

Reaching out, David lifted the girl into his arms. "Gwen. He is still alive, but," he paused, "Dr. Meyer says it is just a matter of time."

"No!" Gwen clutched him in a strangle hold, and he had to unlace her hands from his neck.

"Gwen, listen to me. You must wipe your tears for Nate's sake. He wants to see you—you too," David added, nodding at Hope. "Gwen, we must not carry on while we're with Nate. Understand?"

Hearing the firmness of her cousin's tone, Gwen nodded. Silently, the three headed downstairs.

Mrs. Forrester stopped the solemn procession. "Every thing's all sixes and sevens. All this fuss. I hear Beaucamp has gone." She smiled at David in a way that turned Hope's stomach. "Now there is nothing standing in the way of the two of you. I think—"

"Enough, madam," David commanded. "You have caused enough uproar in this family. Since, as you say, your daughter's future is now in my hands, I suggest you go to your room and stay there. If you cause the least bit of trouble, I shall personally escort you from the premises. Is that clear?"

Blanching, Hope's mother opened and closed her mouth, reminding Hope sharply of a fish. Clamping her mouth shut, Mrs. Forrester slunk back to her chambers.

In Nate's large bedchambers done in shades of russet and forest green, Celeste sat in a chair, staring unseeing toward the far wall. The new duke held his duchess, who wept silently in his arms. Setting Gwen down beside the bed, David stepped back. Hope would have followed David, but Gwen grasped her hand so hard she couldn't free herself.

"Nate?" Gwen touched her brother's pale cheek.

He managed a weak smile. "Poppet. I am glad you are here."

"Oh, Nate, can you forgive me for all the horrid things I said?" she cried, flinging herself onto his chest.

Nate grimaced and sucked in a breath with such difficulty that Hope hauled the girl back. Nate flashed Hope a look of gratitude. "Poppet, of course I forgive you. I love you."

"They say you are going to die. Are you?" Gwen asked with her little-girl directness.

"I fear so, Poppet." He struggled for breath.

"But you don't know Jesus. Nate, you have to know Jesus." Once more Hope had to hold the girl back. Faith came to take the hysterical girl from the bed.

Hope turned to go, but Nate stopped her. "Hope, please."

"Yes, Nate?"

"I am. . .sorry for. . .everything."

"I know."

"I love them, you know. All of them. I told them so."

"I am sure they know that."

"Is there hope for me?" Seeing her expression, he shook his head, grimaced, spoke. "No, not here. I know I am dying—but I am not ready. After all I've done, brought Beaucamp home and all. Do you. . ." He sucked in a breath, coughed. "Will Jesus still forgive someone like me?"

Unable to hold back her tears, Hope let them run unchecked down her cheeks. "Oh, yes, Nathaniel. Oh yes. He loves you so much."

"Will you. . .help me, Hope?"

Taking Nate's hand in hers, quietly, tearfully, Hope bowed her head.

❧

Instead of one funeral, there were two. The Glynis and Fairen families arrayed in black solemnly mourned their dead with pain, yet with the peace of knowing that one day they would be together again. They could find joy that in death Nate had found life.

Emily proved a treasure in those days, organizing the household, releasing the sisters and mother to grieve. Carter berated himself for not doing more for his son and was filled with guilt at his sense of relief that Jonathan would now inherit. Celeste became quieter, mature before her years, but Gwen was hit hardest of all.

No smile lit the small face, and all her energetic joy of life disappeared as though erased. Day by day, she clung to Hope. Her world was a void without emotion, without feeling, without life. Hope scarcely ate or slept in her concern for the girl.

A week later, David came to visit Hope. She walked into his open arms.

"My Hope." His lips found hers. Finally, Hope had come home.

"David, I have missed you." She snuggled in the warmth of his arms. "I thought. . ."

He stared down into her face. "I love you, Hope. That's all you need know. I love you."

"And I love you."

His face lit up at her passionate declaration. "My beautiful Hope," he murmured to her surprise. Just as suddenly, he released her and took her hand, excitement shining in his loving gaze. "Come. Everything is set, my Hope. Now there is time for you and me."

"But Gwen—"

"Mrs. Haskle will see to her. You'll see her soon."

David led Hope to her room and Jenny's ministrations. A hot bath did wonders for her exhaustion, and the white-and-silver gown Jenny fastened her into aroused Hope's curiosity. Jenny only smiled.

It was the new duke himself who came to escort her to dinner, and Hope was vaguely disappointed until she realized they headed not toward the dining room, but toward the chapel.

With a slight smile, the duke escorted her up the aisle to where David, standing next to the vicar, waited for his bride. Out of the corner of her eye, Hope saw her mother wiping her eyes several pews behind her grace and Mrs. Barrington.

At the altar, Celeste handed Hope a single red rose, while on the other side, Jonathan winked. Scarcely able to see through her tears, Hope took David's hand, and they pledged themselves to each another.

Sitting side by side in the pew, Carter squeezed Faith's hand. "I love you, now and always," he whispered.

"And I, you, Carter."

Lord and Lady Thorwall held the reception at Thorn Hall. Mrs. Forrester, however, left as soon as the ceremony was over in a post chaise, saying she had received an invitation from a friend to visit. Hope was not to know, but David had prompted the woman's departure, in order to spare his bride more of her mother's embarrassing manipulations.

After the simple, but lovely reception, David took Hope's hand to lead her from Thorn Hall.

"You're leaving me?" Gwen wailed.

"Only for a short while, Gwen," David told her gently.

Disconcerted, Hope went to the girl and held her close. "Gwen, mayhap," her eyes pleaded with the others to understand, especially David, "after we return from the honeymoon, you can visit me every day for awhile."

"Yes, Gwen. Hope will not be gone long," David assured her.

Lady Thorwall came up with the perfect solution. "Why can't Gwen stay with us for awhile?"

Faith hesitated, then nodded. "All right. Gwen, you may stay."

For the first time since Nate's "accident," Gwen smiled.

Emily, looking on, wiped a tear as memories flooded back

of the death of her mother-in-law and Faith's father. "Gwen," she sniffed, "mayhap one day you can visit us in America. Though I must soon return home, I will be waiting to hear from you."

"One day," Gwen breathed as though taking a vow. "One day, I shall go to America."

Meeting David's tender gaze, Hope smiled. As they headed toward the waiting carriage, Hope breathed a prayer of thanks that for Gwen there was hope and a bright future, just as at last there was for her.

A Letter To Our Readers

Dear Reader:

In order that we might better contribute to your reading enjoyment, we would appreciate your taking a few minutes to respond to the following questions. When completed, please return to the following:

Rebecca Germany, Managing Editor
Heartsong Presents
P.O. Box 719
Uhrichsville, Ohio 44683

1. Did you enjoy reading *Where There is Hope*?
   - ❑ Very much. I would like to see more books by this author!
   - ❑ Moderately
     I would have enjoyed it more if ______________

     ____

2. Are you a member of **Heartsong Presents**? ❑Yes ❑No
   If no, where did you purchase this book? ______________

   ____

3. What influenced your decision to purchase this book? (Check those that apply.)

❑ Cover	❑ Back cover copy
❑ Title	❑ Friends
❑ Publicity	❑ Other______________

4. How would you rate, on a scale from 1 (poor) to 5 (superior), the cover design? ______________

5. On a scale from 1 (poor) to 10 (superior), please rate the following elements.

___Heroine ___Plot

___Hero ___Inspirational theme

___Setting ___Secondary characters

6. What settings would you like to see covered in **Heartsong Presents** books?________________________

____

____

7. What are some inspirational themes you would like to see treated in future books?________________

____

____

8. Would you be interested in reading other **Heartsong Presents** titles? ❑ Yes ❑ No

9. Please check your age range:
❑ Under 18 ❑ 18-24 ❑ 25-34
❑ 35-45 ❑ 46-55 ❑ Over 55

10. How many hours per week do you read? __________

Name ____
Occupation ____________________________________
Address _______________________________________
City ______________ State __________ Zip __________